RARE

NICO'S HEART

DAWN SULLIVAN

Published by Dawn Sullivan

Cover Design: Kari Ayasha-Cover to Cover Designs

Photographer: Shauna Kruse-Kruse Images & Photography

Model: Bryan Monville

Language: English

I want to thank all of my family and friends for their support throughout this new journey.

A big thank you to Angie for inspiring me and encouraging me to actually start my journey to become the author I want to be. And to Kathy and Jaeka for staying up all night letting me bounce ideas off of them.

I hope everyone enjoys reading Nico's Heart as much as I enjoyed writing it.

A ngel was sitting on the enclosed back porch watching the rain fall. She had always loved the rain. It gave her a feeling of peace and comfort in a world where she normally had none. As she listened to the sounds of her team in the kitchen, she thought about the mission they had just returned from. They were gone four and a half weeks this time. It normally wouldn't have taken so long, but the cartel had been paranoid. Just when she thought they were getting close, they would come up empty because the hostage would be relocated. Even with all of their special abilities, it took them awhile to track down the cartel and steal back the senator's son. Angel's team never gave up though, and after weeks of traipsing through the jungle, they were finally back home and needed some major downtime.

Angel smiled as she listened to Nico give Rikki a hard time about missing a shot out in the jungle. Everyone knew he was teasing. Rikki never missed. She always hit her target, no matter what the conditions were like. Rikki and Trace were a couple of the best snipers Angel had ever seen, and she was glad they were on her team. Angel and her crew were in the 'search and retrieval' business. They called themselves RARE, which stood for Rescue and Retrieval Extractions, and contracted out to several different agencies who contacted them when they were needed. RARE took on the missions no one else wanted. Each member of her team had a special ability that helped them become the best extraction team out there. Most had more than one, like Angel. No one outside of their circle needed to know what those abilities were, unless for some reason, the team members chose to share certain information. Otherwise, as far as Angel was concerned, it was confidential. And by confidential, she meant the 'I could tell you but then I would have to kill you' kind. All anyone else needed to know was that RARE did not stop until the job was done.

"Phone's ringing, boss," Nico hollered, right before Angel's phone went off. Not recognizing the number, Angel thought about letting the call go to voice mail. "Answer it," she heard Nico say from behind her. Well shit, this couldn't be good if Nico was telling her to take the call. None of them were ready to go back out on a mission, and had all agreed to take the next couple of weeks off. Damn him and his premonitions.

As she put the phone to her ear, she turned toward Nico and flipped him off with a grin. "This is Angel."

"My name is Jenna Montgomery," a soft voice said. "I need your help. Please." Angel's eyes narrowed when Nico's hands curled into fists at his sides, and a low growl rumbled in his chest. What the hell was going on?

Her team slipped into the room, surrounding her and

Nico, and Angel switched the phone to speaker so they could all hear the conversation. "I'm listening, Jenna. Tell me what's going on."

"She's gone," Jenna cried, her breath catching on a sob. "She's gone, and no one can find her. They've tried. They have done everything that they can think of, but they can't find her. God, please, you have to help me. You have to get my daughter back!"

Daughter? Angel felt the familiar pain swamp her, but gritted her teeth and pushed it aside. There wasn't room for her ghosts in this conversation. "How did you get my number, Ms. Montgomery? Have you contacted the appropriate authorities?" Very few people had her direct line. All calls went into a voice mail that was kicked to Angel's cell phone. Her privacy was important to her, and she only shared her direct number with her team and a handful of others who needed it.

"Jeremiah Black gave it to me." Jenna's voice wavered, and she whispered, "Please, help me. Lily was taken over forty-eight hours ago. I overheard one of the enforcers say that the trail has gone cold. I need you."

If Jeremiah Black had given out her personal information to someone without letting her know first, then the situation had already reached a point where no one else would be able to help. RARE had gone on several missions for Jeremiah, and her team both liked and respected him. He worked for the FBI, and he was also a grizzly bear shifter, which meant this call was shifter related. Not only that, but Jenna was right. The first forty-eight hours were the most critical. "What have the authorities said?" Angel tried once again.

Jenna seemed to hesitate before replying, "I am a wolf

shifter with the White River pack. My brother, Chase Montgomery, is the alpha. I haven't told him that I am contacting you, yet. He doesn't know about you and your team, and until you promise me you will help, he won't. Chase and his enforcers have tried everything that they can think of, and still they cannot find Lily. Will you come?"

Angel cocked her head, her eyes once again straying to Nico. He stood in front of her, a deep growl rising in his throat, his eyes fixated on the phone she held. What the hell was his problem? They had dealt with child kidnappings numerous times, and he had never acted this way before. He needed to get control of his wolf, and fast. The missing child was their top priority.

Technically, something like this was shifter business. Not hers. They had a shifter council that was to be contacted and informed about what was taking place before Angel and her team could be called in. Angel had actually worked with them in the past on a couple of cases, so she knew what hoops she would have to jump through, but there was a child involved. There was no way in hell RARE was going to stand down at this point. Angel would jump through as many hoops as she needed to, but they were going after that little girl.

"Does the council know what's going on?" she asked Jenna.

"They know that Lily was taken, and they have been actively involved in the search for her. They sent two of their own enforcers to help."

"Okay," Angel finally agreed, knowing she had no choice, "I will get in touch with the council and let them know of my intentions to assist your pack. As long as they give their permission, I will help. Where do we meet your alpha?"

"Jeremiah said you were close to us. Do you know where the White River Wolves compound is?"

"Yes."

"Come to the compound. I will let the guards at the gate know to let you right in. Please, hurry," Jenna said. The compound was about five miles outside of Boulder, a good forty minutes from Angel's place. It was where the local wolf pack lived on acres and acres of land, where they could shift and run without fear of being hunted. Well, until now, it would seem.

"Jenna, make sure the guards know that we will be coming fully armed, and we will not leave our weapons at the gate. If you want our help, they will let us through. Also, everyone needs to understand, once we take over the case, it is ours. No one can interfere. I know they will want to keep looking, but it is not an option. They will all stand down, or we will walk."

There was complete silence on the other end of the line for a full minute, and then Jenna replied, "It won't be a problem. When you come in the compound, take a left and go to the very first building. The enforcers are meeting in a conference room on the second floor, down at the end of the hall. They will get you all of the information that you need. And I'll talk to my brother before you arrive so he knows I hired you. Money is not an issue. You will be paid whatever your standard fee is."

As Angel ended the call, she wondered what she had just gotten her team into. It was obvious by Jenna's hesitant response that she had no idea how she was going to get her brother to back off when RARE stepped in and took over. Chase Montgomery was an alpha. Alpha males did not just give up and step aside. Especially in something that involved family and pack. However, in this case, he was not going to have a choice. After Angel's team took over, anything Chase and his enforcers did could negatively affect the final outcome, and Angel was not willing to let that happen. It didn't matter, though. None of them would leave a child out there. They would hunt her down and bring her home no matter what it took. As she looked around at her team, Angel did not say a word. One nod was all it took, and they all left to pack their bags and collect their gear. There would not be any rest for them tonight, but they didn't care. A child's life was way more important. As far as they were concerned, they could rest when they were dead.

Chase stared blankly out of the window at the beautiful landscaping in the back of his office building. All he could think about was Lily. She was the princess of the wolf pack, born to his sister six years ago. No one knew who the father was, and Jenna refused to tell anyone. He'd asked many times, just so that he could hunt the bastard down and kill him slowly. All he knew was that Jenna had been out with some friends at a club one night, and had decided to leave early. Instead of having someone walk her to her car, his sister left on her own, and was jumped in the parking lot. Nine months later, Lily was born. Jenna refused to talk about it. She was afraid if the man somehow found out about Lily, he would come after both of them. Had he somehow found out anyway and grabbed Lily? Chase had no idea. None of their leads had panned out. His best trackers were unable to find her. He didn't know where to go from here, but there was no way he was going to give up. His niece was out there, probably hurt and terrified. He would hunt for her with his last breath. It was time to make Jenna come clean about that night. He didn't want to hurt her, but anything she might remember could possibly help them find Lily.

Chase turned at the knock on his open door. His sister stood there hesitantly, her hand raised to knock again. Absently, he wondered how many times she had knocked already and he hadn't heard.

"Chase, I need to talk to you about something," Jenna said tentatively, "but I need you to have an open mind." He saw the nervousness in her eyes, heard it in her voice, but she went on. "It's about Lily. I have a way to get her back, and I need you to listen."

Chase stiffened, but he was willing to listen to anything that could help them find Lily. "Go on."

"Jeremiah Black told me about an extraction team that he has worked with in the past. He says they are the best of the best. They can find anyone, anywhere. He has no idea how they do it, but when they have nowhere else to turn, they call in RARE. He thinks they might have some special abilities that help them." The last was said very softly, with Jenna staring at his chest.

"Abilities?"

"Psychic abilities," she rushed out. "Jeremiah said there isn't any other explanation for it, but the group is very closed-mouthed about everything, so he doesn't know for sure."

"I don't give a fuck how they do what they do. If they can find my niece, bring them here," Chase demanded.

Jenna's eyes widened in shock, but she nodded quickly. "There is one more thing," she said quietly. "If they do accept my request to look for Lily, which it sounds like they will as long as the council approves it, you and all of your enforcers have to back off, Chase. You can't be involved. Angel, the person in charge, said that if you are not willing to step aside and let them do their jobs, then they will walk. You have to let them try, Chase. For me. For Lily."

Chase stood in silence, watching Jenna for a moment as he thought about it, but in the end there was only one decision he could make. "Fine. I am willing to give them forty-eight hours to do what they can do without any involvement on our end. If they have gotten further than us after that time is up, then they can continue. If not, I start looking again."

Jenna looked up at him in surprise. "Really?"

"I don't know what else to do, Sis," he whispered. "We have exhausted all of our leads. We have to find her, and I will use any means necessary to do that. But, you need to understand something, Jenna. They are going to need to know everything, and I mean everything, if they are going to be able to help."

Jenna nodded and grabbed his arm, grasping it tightly. "I know. I will do anything for my daughter, Chase. I only want to tell the story once, though. Angel and her team are meeting us in the conference room as soon as they can get here. Let's go tell everyone what's going on so the pack isn't surprised when RARE shows up."

Nico Marx struggled to get his emotions under control as they pulled up to the guard station at the compound, but it was hard. His wolf wanted to get to Jenna now. Jenna and Lily were his, dammit. He knew it. Had known the moment he heard Jenna's voice. And while they were sitting around playing patty cake with the fucking guards, his Jenna was somewhere in the compound in pain. He could not stop the low growl that emerged as he watched the guards.

Angel sent him a glare. "Nico," she demanded in a low voice, "what the hell is your problem? Knock your shit off!"

Nico glared right back, for the first time in all of the years he had worked for Angel refusing to back down. "Get us in there now," he growled. Angel's eyes narrowed, but then she turned back to the guards, smiled sweetly, and blew them a kiss as she drove through the gates.

As soon as the SUV stopped in front of the office building, Nico jumped out.

"Not so fast, Turbo," Angel yelled. "Get your ass over here."

Nico swore under his breath as he walked around the vehicle to his boss. "Look, I'm sorry," he started to say, but Angel stopped him with a hand on his arm.

"Talk to me, Nico," she said softly. "Who is she to you?"

"Mine," he replied gruffly. "She and Lily are mine."

Angel was used to his premonitions, so she only eyed him for a moment before turning away as she said, "Come on, Caveman, let's go get back what's yours."

The conference room was huge and filled with people already. Angel and her team walked right in and over to a table that was in one corner. Jaxson, their resident tech geek, pulled out his laptop, gearing it up so that it was ready to go, as Angel clapped her hands loudly and yelled, "Listen up, everyone. My name is Angel, and this is my team. As of right now, this case is ours. I need everything you have on it and I need it yesterday. I want to know where, when, why, and how. Exactly where and when was Lily taken? Do you have any ideas on who could have taken her and why? How the hell did they get to her? What guards were asleep on the fucking job that day, because you can't tell me that the alpha's niece doesn't have enforcers watching her every move. I want to talk to them. If she was taken from within the compound, then you have a traitor and we will find that person. If you have questions for me, they can wait. I want mine answered first. As everyone knows, the first forty-eight hours are the most critical. It's been over that, and I'm sorry, but we do not have time to sit and play nice right now."

As all talking ceased and everyone stared at her, there

was movement at the door. A large man standing well over six feet, with short black hair, and the clearest blue eyes she had ever seen, stood in the doorway. Next to him was a beautiful, petite woman. This was definitely the alpha, Chase. She could tell by the power that surrounded him, radiating off of him in waves, and by the pain in his eyes. Pain that she would do whatever it took to erase. And just where had that thought come from?

The woman with him was obviously Jenna. She had long black hair that touched the middle of her back, and blue eyes that matched her brother's.

"Angel," he said, nodding his head to her, "I'm Chase Montgomery, and this is my sister, Jenna. Please forgive my people. They haven't been told of this new development, yet. Everyone will give you their complete cooperation. I have been informed of your requirements regarding taking our case and I agree to give you forty-eight hours to see what you can do without any involvement on our end, and then we will go from there."

"You'll give us the time we need. We will find Lily no matter how long it takes, and you will not interfere," Nico growled.

Angel gritted her teeth, knowing that challenging the alpha was definitely not the way to go. As Chase's eyes narrowed on Nico, she hissed out of the side of her mouth, "Back off, Asshat."

Suddenly, Jenna gasped as she moved slowly into the room, her eyes on Nico. "Mate," she whispered. Great, things just kept getting better and better.

J enna stood in front of her mate, her eyes wide with shock. Her mate was there...he was really there. He was gorgeous, with short dark hair, captivating green eyes, and muscles she wanted to reach out and trace with her fingertips. Jenna closed her eyes and inhaled deeply, taking in the delicious spicy scent that was all him. That was how she had known he was hers. Her wolf started pushing at her to get to him at the very first whiff. Before that, she had barely moved since the first twenty-four hours after Lily was taken. At first, she was mad as hell and had gone crazy trying to find her, but the longer Jenna had been without Lily, the more withdrawn and depressed her wolf had become.

How could he be here now? Now, when her daughter was missing and they didn't have time to enjoy the knowledge that they had really found each other? Some people searched their whole lives for their true mate, but never found them. Some mated with others who were not their true mate because being alone was just too hard. But her mate was here, right now, within reach. He was here, and he was going to help find Lily. As happy as she was, she dreaded it, too, because now, in front of everyone, she would have to talk about that night. The night her precious little girl was conceived.

As Jenna and her mate stared at each other, Angel took control of the situation, diverting the attention away from them. "Come on, people! Get me that information I asked for, now!"

One enforcer spoke up quickly, "Lily was taken from inside the compound around 10 a.m. on Monday. She was at the playground playing with friends. Jenna was working, so one of the older pups had Lily that day. There were the standard two guards at the gate and two female enforcers were at the playground watching over the children."

"I want names," Angel demanded.

"Aiden and Xavier were on the gate," the enforcer responded. "Sable and Selene were the enforcers at the playground. The pup that took Lily is Callie. She's nineteen and goes to college. Callie helps out with the children when she has time."

"And you are?" Angel asked, raising an eyebrow.

"My name is Bran Delaney, Ma'am, the beta of our pack."

Nodding to him, she glanced around the room. "Okay, we have the when and where taken care of. Alpha, I am going to need every person that was just mentioned pulled into different rooms in this building. My team and I will talk to them each separately. Now, we need to work on who and why. I want a list of names of anyone you can think of that would want to take Lily, along with why you think they would want her. Money, payback, maybe a grudge. Whatever it is, I need to know about it. Don't hold anything back."

Jenna tried to keep up as she watched Angel in action. She had never seen anyone like her before. It was obvious this was not the first time Angel and her team had done something like this. She had jumped in and taken charge like she was born to do it. For the first time since Monday, Jenna started to feel hope.

Glancing over at her mate, she saw that he was watching everyone in the room closely. Checking for their responses, she assumed. Her mate. God, she just couldn't get over it. But would he want her once he heard what she had to tell them? In her mind, Jenna knew that what had happened hadn't been her fault, but it did not change the fact that she felt ugly and dirty after what had been done to her. And would he want Lily when he found out who her father was? Lily was nothing like that monster. She was the kindest, sweetest, most caring little girl Jenna had ever known. But, would that matter to the man standing in front of her?

Chase and Bran were over by Jaxson telling him everyone they could think of that had something against Chase as alpha. They were going into details as to why, and what their motives might be. Chase and his enforcers had already been through all of this numerous times, but they knew that if RARE was going to help, they would need all of the information, also. Angel was listening to them as she read some notes that were on a white board at the front of the room. Sable and Selene stood off to the side waiting to be taken into a room for questioning. Two of the other enforcers had gone to the gate to relieve Aiden and Xavier of their duties so that they could come in and answer questions. Callie had been in the middle of a class at the college, but she was now on her way back to the compound.

Nico's gaze was on Jenna, watching her as she stood in silence by the window, not liking the vibes she was giving off. She was obviously scared and upset because of Lily, but he could tell that something else was wrong. Damn, she was so beautiful. And she was in so much pain. He wanted to go over to her and just hold her. To tell her that everything would be okay. That he would fix it. He was an alpha male. They fixed things. Finally, he gave into the need and crossed over to her. Instead of pulling her into his arms like he wanted, he just stood beside her, letting his wolf soak up her presence. She calmed him by just being near, and he was hoping his presence did the same for her.

"Hey, Jenna," he finally said, unable to stand her silence any longer, "my name's Nico." Jenna turned and looked up at him with her beautiful blue eyes full of tears. "I'm going to find her, Jenna. I'm going to find her and bring her home to you. Nothing is going to stop me," Nico promised.

"I believe you," she whispered. She was quiet for a moment, and then she stiffened as she said, "Nico, there is someone else that needs to be on that list. Lily's father. I need to tell everyone about Lily's father."

As she looked at him with scared, pain-filled eyes, Nico thought, Oh, hell no. Whatever had her this upset, it was not something he wanted everyone in the room to know about. "Come on," he said holding out his hand to her. "You can tell me, and afterwards, I will talk to my team."

"But, shouldn't everyone know?" she asked.

"Only my team needs to know everything," he told her. "We just took over, remember?"

"Yeah," she whispered, "but it would probably be best if I told your team all at once, and I know Chase will want to be there. I've…I've never told him what happened. I can do this, Nico. For Lily, I can do anything."

Determination filled her gaze, and Nico knew that she wasn't going to back down. She loved her daughter, and would do whatever was necessary, to help bring her home. "My team and your alpha, but no one else," Nico decided. He respected her wishes, but he was also going to protect her. Silently, she put her hand in his and let him lead her over to where Angel stood.

Angel looked up as they neared, focusing on Nico. Nico glanced around the room, before he whispered into her mind, *Something's wrong with her, Angel. She's upset and scared, but I don't think it is just about Lily. She says she needs to tell us about Lily's father. I don't want anyone hearing whatever she has to say except the team and Chase. I can already tell I am going to gut the bastard."* Angel glanced away, acting as if she was reading the notes again as she responded, *We will take care of your mate, Nico. I promise."*

Everyone on the team was telepathic. It was one of Angel's requirements for a team member, and it came in really handy when they were out on an op. Another requirement was that you had to be a badass. So, when Nico said he was going to gut the bastard, he meant it.

"Jenna needs to tell us about Lily's father," Nico said out loud. Before he could continue, a young, very upset girl came through the door.

"Callie," Chase said, walking toward them, "thank you for coming. We need to talk to you about Lily and the day she went missing."

"I'm so sorry I didn't watch her more closely, Alpha," Callie cried, her eyes welling up with tears. "I left her near the slide to go help one of the other children on the swings. I wasn't gone for very long, I swear!"

"I know, Callie. We have a new team helping us find

Lily now. They need you to tell them everything that you can remember. Don't leave anything out," Chase ordered.

"Yes, Alpha. Anything for Lily," she said. She turned toward Jenna, "I really am sorry, Jenna. So sorry!"

Nico pulled Jenna closer to his side when he felt her tense up. He sent a look to Angel, who once again took charge.

"One of my team members will take each of you into a room to ask you some questions privately. Aiden, you're with Rikki. Xavier is with Trace. Sable, you go with Phoenix. Callie, you will talk with Jaxson. Selene, you're with me. Let's get this done," Angel ordered. When Nico looked at her in confusion, she told him, "I need you to take Jenna to her house quickly, and get whatever Lily loves the most there. A blanket, a pillow, a favorite teddy bear. Whatever it is, get it and bring it right back here." Realizing what she was going to do, he nodded in understanding, and pulled Jenna out of the room.

"Come on, everyone. Let's get this done!" Angel ordered. As they all filed out of the room, Nico saw Angel glance back at Chase, who gave her a quick nod, his face a blank mask. She returned his nod and took off.

———

IT WAS cold and dark when Lily opened her eyes. She was so hungry. She hadn't eaten anything since the snack Callie had given her before she went to the park. And she was scared, so scared. She missed her mommy so much. Sometimes she closed her eyes just to imagine that her mommy was there with her, cuddling her close and singing her favorite song.

Lily didn't know where she was. Or where her friend was. They were supposed to be getting a special flower for her mommy, but that never happened. Now Lily was with some men. Mean, scary men. She remembered them throwing her in the back of a van as she screamed and cried for her mommy and Uncle Chase. Someone smacked her, telling her to shut up. Lily had crawled back into the side of the van away from him and held onto her face where it hurt, whimpering. No one had ever hit her like that before. One of the men turned to her and said, "Once we get you to the boss man, you will be his problem. Until then, sit there with your mouth shut unless you want some more of what you just got." As she thought about her Mommy again and how much she missed her, Lily curled into a ball on the hard floor and cried softly until she finally fell back to sleep.

6

The interviews were over within thirty minutes. Angel had trained her team well, and they knew time was of the essence. They needed to gather as much information as possible quickly, and then move on. As soon as they were finished and everyone was back in the conference room, Angel shut the door behind her, locking them all in. Nico and Jenna had arrived just moments before and were talking to Chase. The two council enforcers, Ryker and Storm, stood by themselves in a corner. She had worked with them in the past and really liked them. If she thought they would leave the council, she would hire them in a heartbeat. She didn't know if they had any other abilities, but she knew for a fact that they were both telepathic.

Briefly connecting with her team, she asked, *Anyone get any suspicious vibes?* After she received an *All clear,* response from all of them, she responded, *Not clear on my end. Selene's in on it. She told Lily they were looking for a flower for Jenna, then took her and handed her off to some sleaze balls. I can't prove it, yet, but if pushed hard enough, she will break.* And she would push. She had council enforcers here, and she would use them. She would do whatever it took to get that child back.

Nico tried to keep a tight hold on his wolf. He wanted to get to Selene and punish her for what she had done to Lily, and he could not stop the growl that vibrated through his chest. He was going to kill the bitch slowly for putting his little girl in harm's way. He may not have met her yet, but Lily was his, just as Jenna was. His mate, his child.

Jenna placed a hand on his chest looking up at him. "What is it?" she whispered. "What's wrong?"

Nico shook his head, staring straight at Angel, the muscle in his jaw ticking. His control was slipping and he needed help fast. Even the soothing touch of his mate wasn't working. His growl was getting louder and louder. All eyes in the room were on him.

Angel motioned for Jaxson and Phoenix to stand in front of the door, saying something softly to them, and then she crossed the room to Nico. Standing in front of him she growled right back. Angel was the alpha of their team. His wolf wouldn't back down to anyone but her. "You will back the fuck off, Nico. You will stand down and let me handle this," she ordered in a low voice.

"My mate, my child," he growled back, baring his fangs in anger.

"Trust me," Angel insisted. "Stand down and let me handle it."

Angel stared him down, still growling low in her throat. It took a while, but he was finally able to reign in his wolf and he stepped back. He nodded his head to Angel letting her know he was once again in control. Punching him in the arm lightly, she said, "Now, let me take out the trash so we can get down to business." She turned toward Storm and Ryker, "Selene is yours, enforcers. Please take her to the council and have her explain her part in all of this."

"What? Wait, what the hell are you doing?" Selene yelled as the two enforcers moved toward her.

"We know you are the one that helped the kidnappers, Selene," Angel said, placing her hands lightly on her hips, cocking one to the side. "I don't have time for your crap, so I am going to let the enforcers take you and get what they can out of you."

As Storm reached for her, Selene yanked away and jumped up over the conference table to try and get to the door. Before she got two feet past the table, Angel grabbed her and swung her around slamming her face first into the table. "You have already pissed me off enough, bitch," Angel growled. "You do not want to push me further. One more move like that, and I'll let Nico at you. Right now, he wants to tear you apart piece-by-piece."

"Look," Selene rasped, struggling to get up, "I only helped them because I needed the money. I have no idea who they are, but they promised me they wouldn't hurt her."

"And you believed them?" Chase looked over at the enforcers, his wolf visibly pushing toward the surface. "Do what Angel says. And when you are finished, the council can decide what to do with her. If she comes back here, I will kill her."

Nodding, Ryker cuffed Selene with silver handcuffs, and headed out the door with Storm right behind them.

Once they were gone, Angel ordered everyone else out of the room except her team, Chase, and Jenna. It was time to get busy, and what she was about to do, she didn't want anyone else to see. She would trust Chase and Jenna with her secrets, because she had no other choice, but no one else. The first thing she needed to find out was who Lily's father was. He was the wild card in the equation, and out of everyone who could have snatched Lily, Angel was leaning toward him. She'd learned to trust her gut over the years, and her gut was screaming at her that somehow, he had found Lily.

7

P hoenix and Jaxson stood guard by the door to make sure no one came back in while everyone else took a seat at the conference table. Jenna knew it was her turn to talk, and for her daughter, she would. She would dredge up the old memories that gave her night terrors some nights and she would share them, for Lily. As Jenna sat with her head bowed, thinking about that night, she felt a hand gently stroke her hair. She calmed as she breathed in the scent of her mate. Would he still want her after he found out about all of the nasty, vile things that had been done to her? Yes, she had to believe that he would. Fate wouldn't have given her a mate just to rip him away again.

Sitting up straight, Jenna stiffened her spine and squared her shoulders, looking at all of them as she began. "Seven years ago, my best friend, Toni, mated with a wolf that lived in California. I hadn't seen her for a year or so after the mating, so I decided to take a vacation and fly out there. I rented a car and stayed in a hotel because I wanted the freedom to go off on my own and do things when they were busy. That, and I didn't want to have to depend on her. We were having so much fun. We went shopping, swam in the ocean, and even went up to the mountains to let our wolves run wild a couple of times. One night we decided to do a bar crawl in Oceanside with some of Toni's friends. We had been up in the mountains that day running for hours, so around midnight I was exhausted. Toni and her friends were still going strong and wanted to stay. I had my own car, so I decided to head back to the hotel to get some rest. What I didn't know was that Walker and his buddies had been stalking me all week, waiting for a chance to snatch me. I was opening my car door when I heard the footsteps. Before I could react, I felt a hand cover my mouth, and someone shoved a needle in my neck, knocking me out."

Jenna paused as she tried to get control over the fear that still gripped her every time she thought about what had happened after that. Finally, she continued, "When I woke up, I was in a small room lying on a bed. My clothes had been removed and my arms were chained to a heavy metal headboard above my head. I saw my clothes were thrown on a chair in the corner of the room. I was so groggy. I could hardly move."

Jenna was interrupted by the growling and snarling in the room. "Stop it," Angel ordered roughly. "Let her get this out."

She looked gratefully at Angel and then went on reluctantly. "I heard the door open, and I closed my eyes quickly, trying to act like I was still out of it. There were three of them. They were arguing about what to do with me. One of them was saying that they needed to leave me alone because in a few hours, I was going to be moved to a place where all of the other test subjects were being held. But Walker told them that he was going to have fun with me first. They knew I was a shifter because the other two were telling Walker that he needed to wait. That the General would want to pair me with someone of his choice. Something about he liked to match the subjects with whomever he thought would be the best fit with their psychic abilities. They said something about me being special because I was a shifter, and he wanted to see if a child of mine would have both a wolf and psychic talents. I didn't have a clue what they were talking about at the time. They argued for a while, but Walker won."

She paused for a moment, tears streaming down her face. "I fought as hard as I could. My hands were tied, but my legs weren't. I kicked and bit and screamed, but in the end, it didn't matter. He beat me and raped me while his buddies cheered him on, and there wasn't a damn thing I could do about it. I passed out after what had to have been an hour or so. When I woke up, Walker was gone, and they had removed my chains. They probably figured I wouldn't be able to crawl out of there if I wanted to after what I went through, but they underestimated my wolf. She pushed and pushed at me to get up off that bed and escape. With her help, I was finally able to get up and get dressed. My keys, money, and license were still in the front pocket of my jeans. They must not have checked them. I remember, when I went to leave the room, one of the men came back through the door. I didn't think, I just grabbed the lamp and beat him over the head with it. Once he was down I just kept hitting him and hitting him until I knew he wouldn't get back up." Biting her lip, she whispered, "He was human, so I probably killed him.

Afterwards, I ran out of the room and down the hall. I stopped and listened, but didn't hear anyone else in the house. Walker and the other guy must have left for some reason. I got out of the house and ran and ran until I was a good three to four miles away, making my way through alleys and back yards, trying to stay as hidden as possible. As soon as I thought it was safe, I ran out into the street and hailed a cab. I had no clue where I was, but the driver took me to my hotel. I asked him to wait while I ran in and grabbed my purse and suitcase, which thank God, was already packed because I was leaving the next day. He dropped me off at the airport and I ran in and went thru all of the security. I waited at the gate for hours for my plane to get there." Raking a hand through her hair, she told them, "I worried for months after everything happened that they knew who I was, but then a couple of years went by, and I decided they didn't, because they never came after me."

Jenna stopped when Nico got up and moved away from her. He let out a roar as he swung around and put his fist through the wall. Chase didn't look much better. She could see the tips of his fangs, and his eyes had gone pure wolf. "Dammit, Jenna," Chase growled. "Why didn't you tell me any of this before? Didn't you trust me?"

"It had nothing to do with me trusting you, Chase. It had everything to do with Lily. Don't you see? I had to keep her safe! I didn't tell *anyone* anything until now. I have no idea who the General is. I don't know where Walker is. I don't know what they planned to do with Lily after she was born. Chase, Lily can do things. Things no one knows about. She can talk to me in my head. We have to be somewhat close to each other for me to hear her, and she can't hear me when I try to talk back, but she can talk to me. And sometimes, she knows things are going to happen before they do. She picked out her favorite green blanket because she said the color was the same as her daddy's eyes. Walker has brown eyes. Brown. I will never forget them." Jenna looked over at Nico, right into his captivating green eyes. "She said that her daddy would be coming soon."

"I read up on psychic phenomena before Lily was born so I would know what to expect," Jenna continued, not waiting for anyone to respond. "I didn't know for sure what Walker or the other men had meant when they talked about psychic abilities, but I didn't know anything at all about it. I figured I had better be prepared, just in case. I found some training techniques that I have been using to help Lily cope with everything, but it's getting harder and harder to help her. I taught her how to build a wall in her mind to try and control the thoughts of others that bombard her, and to try and block anyone from getting in her mind that shouldn't be there. She is getting stronger, but she's only six. I honestly don't know if she is able to actually keep someone out of her thoughts. Obviously, I didn't have anyone to test it with."

"Well," Angel said, "there's no time like the present to find out. Get me the blanket and wolf that belong to Lily."

When Jenna looked at her in confusion, Nico turned and explained, "Angel is going to try to connect with Lily. She is the strongest of us here. It's easier if she actually knows the person, but since she's never met Lily, she needs something of hers to help her connect with the child."

"Yes," Angel agreed, "but with Lily having abilities of

her own, it might be easier to connect with her than I thought it would be. Unless she somehow blocks me. No matter what happens, you need to stay away from me and stay quiet. If you talk to me or touch me, it could break whatever connection we might have."

8

L ily slowly woke to a pushing sensation in her mind. No, she thought, struggling against the intrusion, I can't let anyone in. Mommy told me not to. But, as hard as she tried, she could not maintain the wall that kept everyone out.

Lily, she heard a voice whisper softly, *It's okay, honey. I'm not trying to hurt you. I'm here with your mommy and we are trying to find you.*

Lily sat up in the dark room clutching her knees to her chest as she whispered back tentatively, *You're with my mommy?*

Yes, honey, I am, the voice replied gently.

What's your name? Lily asked, unsure whether or not to believe her.

My name is Angel, and I'm helping your mother and Uncle Chase look for you. Lily, do you have any idea where you are? Are you still in Colorado?

I was on a plane, Lily said softly, deciding to trust the

woman. *And it's really cold here now. There's snow. Lots and lots of snow. I'm scared. I want my mommy. And my blanky.*

I know, sweetheart, Angel murmured, *and I'm holding your blanky right now. I also have your little wolf.*

His name is Shadow, Lily whispered. *My daddy had a puppy named Shadow. He was all black.*

Really? Angel asked.

Lily smiled faintly, *Yep. My daddy is coming to get me.*

You better believe he is, sweet girl. He's sitting right here beside me, and he's coming with me to find you, Angel told her.

Lily started to cry, wanting to believe her. *Promise?*

Oh, yes, I promise, Angel told her. *I have to go now, Sweetheart, but you lay back down and rest. We will be there just as soon as we can.*

No, don't leave me! Lily screamed. *Please, don't go!*

I'm so sorry, Lily, but I can't help it. We will come for you. I promise. Now, go to sleep.

Lily slowly drifted off to sleep after a slight push from Angel, dreaming of her daddy and mommy, wishing they were with her now.

NICO WATCHED Angel come back to them with a start. She looked straight at him and said, "Please tell me you had a black puppy named Shadow at some point."

"Yeah, I had him for years. He passed away right before I went into the Marines. Why?" he asked in confusion.

Handing him the wolf, a small smile crossed her lips. "Meet Shadow, named after Lily's daddy's puppy."

"Oh! You got through? You talked to my Lily?" Jenna

cried, her eyes bright with tears. "You're right. She named him Shadow."

"I did. She is all right for now. I got the impression that she's cold, hungry, and scared. She is alone in a dark room with a cement floor, probably a basement. Jaxson, she said that she is in a place that has a lot of snow. She had to fly there. Get online and look for any flight plans out the day Lily was taken and I want to know of any private planes that went somewhere that has a ton of snow. I know they may not always file flight plans, but I'm praying we get lucky. If not, check to see what states just had a bunch of snow dropped and we will go from there. Nico, contact the hangar and tell them to have our plane fueled and ready for takeoff. I want to be wheels up yesterday!"

Jaxson immediately grabbed his laptop, his fingers flying over the keys, as Nico made the call to the hangar.

"I want to go," Chase growled, his hands closing tightly into fists.

"No, Chase. I'm sorry. I wasn't kidding when I told you that you have to stay out of it once we took over. I'm sorry, but it could affect the outcome if you go barreling in. Besides, you need to be here for Jenna. She's going to need someone, and I need Nico with me." It was obvious that Chase was pissed, but he just nodded and walked over to the window, his back to them.

Angel glanced at her watch. It was just after 9 p.m., and thankfully, the rain had stopped a long time ago. It was pitch black outside, but RARE worked best in the dark. It was easier to get in and out undetected. The darkness was their friend in situations like this.

Nico hung up his phone, looking over at her. "The plane will be ready to go in thirty minutes."

"I got something, boss," Jaxson hollered, as he started packing up his toys and putting them away quickly. "Let's move out and I'll tell you on the way."

Nico walked over to Jenna, taking the blanket and Shadow from her. He gently cupped her cheek and leaned down to kiss her softly, once on the forehead and then on the lips. "I will bring her home to you, mate. No matter what, I will bring her home." He gave her a hard hug and turned to follow his teammates out the door.

Angel crossed the room to where Chase stood by the window. Placing a hand on his arm, she told him, "We will be back soon, Chase. Jenna has my number. Get it from her and text me so I have yours, please."

Chase looked down at her and nodded. As she turned to walk away, he grabbed her and yanked her back. Burying his face in her neck, he breathed in deeply as he growled, "Be safe, my Angel."

Angel's eyes widened when she inhaled his scent. Holy shit, this couldn't be happening. Taking one last look at him, Angel turned and ran.

9

"A flight plan was filed by a small private plane on Monday, leaving Denver International at noon and heading to Sioux Falls, South Dakota," Jaxson told the team, as they sped out of the compound and onto the gravel road that would take them to the highway. "There was a blizzard in Sioux Falls that day that closed down the airport from 7 p.m. on. It is the only private plane that landed there before that time. It has to be it."

"How long will it take to get there?" Angel asked.

"A normal private plane, approximately two and a half hours or so. Our jet cruises at around 460 knots, so we should be there in just under an hour," Jaxson answered.

"Make it happen," Angel told him.

Nico sat in the passenger seat with a tight hold on Lily's wolf. She had named him Shadow after her daddy's puppy. She knew him. *I don't even have a picture of her*, he thought, but as he closed his eyes, the vision came to him. It was of him pushing Lily on a swing. Her long black hair was flying in the wind, and she was looking back at him, laughing. Her little dimples were peeking out on each cheek, with her blue eyes shining. She was the perfect image of her beautiful mother. Jenna was there too, sitting under a tree, smiling as she watched them. She had a picnic basket beside her, and as he watched, she called out to them to come and eat.

Nico jerked back to the present with a growl. He was going to have that. He had never had a vision that didn't come true, so he knew that he was going to have that. But he also knew that he was going to have to fight for it. And he would.

As they pulled up to the airstrip, they all jumped out of the SUV and ran to the plane that was loaded and ready to go. They quickly got in and tossed their gear down, Jaxson and Phoenix going up front to pilot the plane. The plan was to get to Sioux Falls, find out where Lily was, extract her, and get back to Denver before anyone had a clue they were in the area. Granted, they had no clue yet where to look once they got there, but they would soon.

"Were you able to find out where the plane is being kept?" she hollered up to Jaxson.

"Yeah, it's in Hangar 12," he yelled back.

"Okay, that's our first stop. We will see what Rikki can get off of it and go from there. Right now, I'm going to check in on Lily."

As the plane coasted down the runway for takeoff, Angel leaned back in her seat and closed her eyes. Right before she went under, she heard Nico demand, "You tell Lily I'm coming for her, Angel. Tell her Daddy will be there soon."

Angel felt Lily waking up when she slipped into her
mind. Lily slowly blinked her eyes open and whispered,
You're back.

As Angel started to respond, there was a noise outside
the door. Lily froze, and Angel gently stroked her hand
through the terrified child's hair. *It's okay, sweetheart. I'm
right here. I promise to stay as long as I can.*

Lily whimpered as she crowded up against the cold
cement wall, shaking. They could hear voices on the other
side of the door, and then it was yanked open. Bright light
came into the room, and Lily squeezed her eyes shut
against the shock and pain. She had been in the dark for
so long that the light was blinding.

The huge man that moved to stand in the middle of
the doorway blocked some of the light and allowed Lily to
adjust to it easier. Still squinting, she tried to make out the
form in front of her, but she was unable to. Angel whispered gently, *Calm down, Lily. Try to get a good look at him
and anyone else you see. Be strong. We are on our way.*

The man came in and roughly grabbed her by the arm,
pulling her out of the dark room and into another, much
brighter one. When she looked up into his cold dark eyes,
one with a scar over the top of it, she felt something warm
and wet slide down her legs. Terror gripped her and she
screamed. She remembered this man from the plane.

As harsh laughter filled the room, Lily tore her gaze
away from the scary man holding her and looked at the
other smaller, but no less scary one. "So you finally found
Walker's kid." The smaller man said.

"Yes, General," the other man replied. "She was living
in a wolf compound with her mother in Colorado. We
stole her right out from under them. Told some stupid

bitch we would give her $100,000 in cash to help us and promised her we wouldn't hurt the girl. Obviously, no money was sent. When the wolves find out her part in it, they will kill her themselves."

The General smiled cruelly, "Good work. Were you followed? Do they have any idea where we are?"

"Nope. The last time our informant checked in, she said they didn't have a clue. That dumbass alpha was running around in circles. They won't find us. Hell, most people probably never heard of Hartford, and we are so far out in the boonies that there is no way they can track us here," the man said confidently.

"Good, that is good," the General replied, his eyes on Lily. "I'm going to head out now. For now, throw her back in her room, but give her some food. I would hate for her to starve to death before we get her to her new home. Bring her to me tomorrow night." As the General walked away, he turned back to look at the other man. "Oh, and Jasper, do not touch her," he said, as an afterthought.

Jasper watched the General leave, cursing when the door shut behind him. Glaring at Lily, he threw her back in the room, slamming the door shut, and she scampered quickly over to the back wall. Angel sat down beside her, and in her mind, she gently pulled Lily onto her lap, cuddling her close and stroking her hair. Lily snuggled closer, crying softly.

He's really scary, Lily whispered. *He wants to do things to me. He wants to hurt me.*

Angel held her tighter and promised, *He won't get the chance, baby girl. Your daddy is coming for you, and once we find you, he won't let anyone hurt you ever again.*

The door opened, and Jasper threw a sack at her. "Eat that," he snarled.

As he was leaving, Lily whispered, "I want my daddy."

Jasper turned around and laughed at her. "Your daddy? Well that ain't gonna happen, girly. I killed that son of a bitch myself. Put a bullet right between his eyes. That's what happens when you cross the General." With that, he turned around and walked out, slamming the door shut behind him.

You lied to me! Lily cried, scrambling away from the wall. *He's dead! My daddy is dead!*

As Lily sobbed, Angel gently put her arms around her again in her mind and firmly said, *Listen to me. Listen!* Lily slowly raised her head, but continued to cry. *Your daddy is with me. He is sitting next to me holding Shadow. The man that Jasper killed is not the same man that you know as daddy. I promise you, Lily.*

Lily sat crying, little hiccups escaping as she tried to get herself under control. She lightly reached out and touched Angel's mind this time, instead of Angel being inside of hers. When she did, she saw her daddy sitting in a seat holding Shadow, looking out the window of an airplane. There was so much pain and sadness in his gaze, but it was her daddy. She knew it. She knew him.

Lily pulled back out of Angel's mind and once again moved up against the wall, clutching the sack of food. Opening up the sack, she felt inside. There was a sandwich, and what felt like an apple. She was so hungry that she inhaled the sandwich in no time, and then started on the apple.

After she had eaten everything, Angel said, *I have to go*

now, Lily. I need to get back to everyone so that we can come and find you.

My Daddy is coming, Lily said softly, as if saying it made it seem more real to her.

Yes, he is, Honey. We will be there to get you just as soon as we can. Lily curled back up on the floor to rest. She was so cold. *Can you shift, Lily? It would keep you warmer.*

I can't. I tried, but I just can't, Lily responded.

Angel nodded her head in understanding. As tired, weak, and upset as Lily was, even if she could shift, she probably would not be able to hold her wolf form for very long. The bastards could at least have given her a blanket. *I will be back,* Angel promised, gently stroking her hair. *Rest now, and your daddy and I will be there soon.* Angel waited a few minutes, making sure Lily was asleep, before leaving her.

The plane was already making its descent when Angel finally came back to them. Nico was going crazy wondering how Lily was. Angel had been gone too long this time. She would be weaker, and they needed her strong to get through this. But, if Angel was gone that long, there was a reason. Which just pissed him off because that meant something was wrong with Lily.

"What happened?" he demanded, as soon as Angel's eyes fluttered open.

"Give me a few minutes, Nico," Angel whispered. She sat quietly with her eyes closed as the plane landed and taxied to Hangar 10, where Jaxson had set it up with a contact he had in the area to have the plane refueled and ready for takeoff.

Once the plane was at a full stop, the team came back and surrounded Angel. She opened her eyes weakly and whispered, "Sorry guys. You are on your own checking out the other plane. I need to rest. Listen up, before I pass out. They have her in a basement. It's an all cement basement. She is locked in a freezing cold, dark room, like a cellar, but she is too weak and scared to shift to get warm. I saw the General. He's a freaky little fucker with bug eyes and wrap-around glasses. He is very powerful though, I can tell. I will have Phoenix do a sketch later. There is a guard with her named Jasper. We need to take that bastard out. He wants to hurt Lily, and not in an 'I want to smack her around' way. More of an 'I'm a sick fucking pig that likes little girls and needs my dick cut off and stuffed down my throat' way." Nico went crazy at that, but she didn't give him time to interrupt her. "They are in some place called Hartford. That's all I got. Go get whatever you can from their plane and get back here." That was all she managed before her eyes drifted shut and she was out cold.

"I'll stay here with Angel," Trace told them. "Go get what you need and get back. I will spot you as much as I can from here." Without waiting for a response, he took out his sniper case, removed his rifle, and began to put it together.

The rest of the team jumped out of the plane and took off toward Hangar 12, hiding in the shadows so that no one could see what they were up to. Weapons drawn and ready, they quietly entered the building and surrounded the small plane. They got the plane door open, and Rikki and Nico slipped inside. Jaxson and Phoenix stood guard outside, one at the door of the hangar and one by the plane.

Nico did a quick sweep through the back of the plane, while Rikki checked the cockpit. Once the plane was cleared, Rikki walked back toward the seats, removing her gloves. Rikki's gift was sometimes a huge pain in the ass. She could touch an object and see who had touched it before, and even catch their thoughts. That was why she always wore light weight gloves. It sucked in the summer, but better than seeing a bunch of sporadic visions from anything and everything she came in contact with.

Unfortunately, her gift wasn't always reliable. Sometimes it took her a lot further back than she needed to go. Sometimes, the reading was so loud, that it sucked her in and it was hard for her to get back to the present. Sometimes, she didn't get jack shit. She had been practicing extensively the past couple of years that she had been on Angel's team, though, and was getting a lot better at controlling it. And she would control it now, she vowed. For Nico, she would. He was like a brother to her. Her team was the only family she had, and she would do anything for them.

Seeing a newspaper sitting on one of the seats, Rikki reached out and touched it. Nothing. Dammit, she would NOT let Nico down. She grabbed a small pillow on another seat. Still nothing.

Her gaze traveling around the small plane, Rikki saw an empty pop can sitting in a holder in one of the chairs on the other side of the aisle. Taking a deep breath, she reached out and lightly touched it. The vision came swift and hard this time. A guy with cold dark eyes and black hair, with a scar running up over one eye, was taking a swig out of the can as he looked at a little girl with long black hair curled up in the corner on the floor. She was watching him, her eyes never leaving his face. He laughed at her loudly. "You want some of this, girly?" he said, crudely grabbing his crotch with one hand. The child's eyes widened in shock and fear, and she pushed herself further into the corner. He just laughed again, taking another drink of his soda. Pulling the food tray down in front of him, he placed a map on it. There was a spot circled on the map. "No one will find us where I am taking you," he told the little girl. "It's so far out in the sticks, I don't even know if I can find it."

As Rikki watched, the man took out a piece of paper and started writing down directions. Holy shit, Rikki thought. This was what she needed. The vision started to fade, but she gritted her teeth and forced it back. South on 38W, left onto East 2nd Street. She committed it all to memory as he wrote it down. Times like this, it came in handy to have a photographic memory. When she was sure she had everything she needed, she let the vision slip away.

Nico watched Rikki as she stood there in a trance. He was going to give it two more minutes and then try and pull her out, but all of a sudden, she shook herself and focused her gaze on him.

"Let's go get your little girl, my brother," she said, throwing a fist pump in the air.

Angel was still out when the team made it back to the plane. As they grabbed their gear, Trace lifted Angel up into his arms, and they moved to the SUV on the side of the hangar that Jaxson had waiting for them. He had contacts everywhere. There wasn't anything he couldn't get if he needed it.

Once they were in the vehicle and on their way, Rikki gave directions to Nico who was driving this time. "A dirt road? Where the hell do they have her?" he growled.

Jaxson paused, looking something up on his phone before glancing up to say, "Less than half an hour away. Before the dirt road, we need to find a place to stash the SUV and go in on foot. It will be about three miles out, but it is safer that way. Otherwise they might see us coming. Looks like an old farmhouse, probably abandoned."

Nico floored it, praying there were no cops around that he would have to deal with. At least the roads had been cleared of all the snow that had been dumped recently.

When they were close, Nico backed the vehicle off the road and into a clump of trees, praying they didn't get stuck. They would have to worry about that later, though. Right now, all that mattered was getting to Lily. As the team geared up, Nico woke Angel. Sitting up, she shook the cobwebs out of her head, and reached for her own weapons.

Angel loved her throwing stars. She put some of them in the side pockets on her pants and a couple up her sleeves and in her coat pockets.

Phoenix liked anything that went boom. He shoved some grenades in his pockets, and put some other goodies in a backpack that would make the place explode when they were done.

Rikki was partial to her knives. She had a special set that the team had made for her that she strapped to the chest harness she put on, two handles up and two down.

Trace's baby was his sniper rifle, but he loved all kinds of guns. He strapped on a Glock to go with the knives and two guns he already had on him.

Nico and Jaxson didn't really have any favorites. They liked it all. Anything that helped kick ass worked for them.

They all put on some night vision goggles and took off toward the old farm house as quickly as possible through the snow. They trained daily for shit like this and could run for miles at this pace. Which was good, because they estimated Lily was being held about three and a half miles away from where they hid the SUV.

When they were about a half a mile out, the team

slowed down and eventually came to a stop. *Okay, let's get a little bit closer so we can get the layout of the place*, Angel ordered.

Carefully, they crept up and fanned out around the house. *One guy inside*, Angel said. *It's that sick bastard, Jasper. We will take him out. Two guys on the South side and two on the North. That's it. They really think they are safe and no one is going to find them out here. Let's prove them wrong. Trace, get on the south side and take out those guards. Rikki, you go to the north side and take care of the others. Let us know as soon as it's done. Then you stand guard out here while Nico, Jaxson, and I go in. Phoenix, set the place to blow while we get Lily out. Let's do this. In and out. Now!*

Trace took off in one direction while Rikki went in the other. There was complete silence for a full two minutes and then Rikki muttered, *Clear*! Five seconds later, Trace said the same. Quickly, Nico and Angel moved up toward the front of the house while Jaxson moved around to the back.

I see a window open back here. No wires. I'm going in, Jaxson told them.

Nico finished picking the lock on the door and eased it open silently. *We're in.*

Jasper was watching TV in the living room. *He's yours, Jaxson*, Angel said. Nico froze. What did she mean he was Jaxson's? That bastard was his! *Lily needs you, Nico. We need to get to her.*

I will do this for you, Nico, Jaxson promised him. *I will take him out slowly and painfully.*

Nico growled lowly, angry that he wasn't the one that was going to end the miserable bastard's life, but then he nodded to Jaxson. Angel was right. Lily needed him, and he trusted his friend to make Jasper pray for death. Nico watched while Jaxson crept into the living room, slipping out a couple of knives. He watched the first slice he placed into the sick bastard, and then turned and took off to find the stairs that would take him to Lily.

LILY HEARD the screams up above and huddled in a ball in the corner of the room, shaking. Suddenly, she heard a noise at her door. There was a loud bang, and then the door slowly opened. As the light shone in on her, she watched the figure of the person that filled the doorway. He opened the door wider and then knelt down. "Lily, come here sweet girl. Come here, my princess. Let's get you home to Mommy."

As her vision adjusted to the light, she saw him for the first time in person. He looked so strong and fierce. It was her daddy. He was alive and real, and he had come for her. She tried to jump up to go to him, but her legs didn't want to work right. So she started crawling. "Daddy, it's really you. You came for me," she cried, sobs racking her body.

He stood up when he saw her crawling, running to her and pulling her off the ground and into his arms. "I'm right here, my little princess. I've got you," he crooned, as he snuggled her close.

"Let's go, Nico," Lily heard a voice say. "We need to get out of here now."

She recognized that voice. "Angel, you came, too. Just like you said you would."

"You better believe it, Sweetheart," Angel said, a wide grin crossing her face. "Now, let's blow this popsicle stand!" Lily let out a small giggle of surprise, as her daddy held her tightly and they took off across the room and up the stairs.

Jaxson met them at the top of the stairs and said, "It's done. Let's get the hell out of here."

They heard the first explosion as they hit the tree line a mile away from the house. Nico pushed Lily's head into his chest and ran as fast as he could to where they had left the SUV. Once the team all made it back to the vehicle, they piled in and took off back toward the airport, Jaxson at the wheel.

Once there, they didn't waste any time getting into the air and on their way back to Colorado. Nico held Lily on his lap as she snuggled Shadow and her special blanket. She was now dressed in clean pink fuzzy pajamas, and she refused to leave his side. He was okay with that, though. His team would pick up his slack because he was family, and Lily was his little girl now, which made her family, too.

As the plane pulled up to their hangar at Denver International, Nico looked over at Angel and asked, "What now, boss?" Someone was still out there trying to get his family. A family that he had just found out about, one he still needed to spend time with and get to know. He could not do that while he was worrying about who was going to come after them next.

"Let's get you and Lily back to Jenna right now. You stay with them at the compound while we all go home and rest. We will be back tomorrow to figure out our next move. I will make sure Chase has enforcers he personally trusts guarding you and yours. Honestly, though, I think we are going to have to go hunting, Nico. They aren't going to leave your family alone unless we take them out," Angel replied.

"True that," Rikki piped up. "We aren't going to let anyone hurt your family, Nico. So, we hunt them down and take out the threat."

As everyone agreed, Nico nodded, running a hand

lightly over Lily's hair. "Let's get back to the compound and rest, but tomorrow we plan. We plan, then we hunt, then we strike."

Exiting the plane, they hurried over and piled into the waiting vehicle, Lily still snuggled in Nico's arms. In less than forty minutes he would have both Lily and Jenna with him. Leaning his head back against the seat, he sighed. He was tired, but all he wanted to do was hold Jenna and Lily close.

Angel was talking to Chase on her cell phone, making plans to have his enforcers guard Nico and his family for the rest of the day and night. He could tell she was exhausted as she hung up the phone. She was going on a couple of days without much sleep, plus she had used her abilities a lot more than normal, but she wasn't done yet. Angel would push herself until she knew that her family was safe. Then, and only then, would she allow herself to crash.

When they arrived at the compound, Angel didn't even pause at the gate. She smiled and waved at the guards, but just kept driving. When they stopped in front of the same building they went to before, the door was flung open and Jenna ran out and down the stairs to the SUV. Nico stepped out of the vehicle, biting back a sound of protest when Jenna pulled Lily from him. His arms felt empty until Jenna leaned into them, holding Lily to her. He wrapped them both in his arms tightly, burying his face in Jenna's neck, inhaling deeply. His mate. He was home.

As ANGEL WATCHED Nico with his family, she felt Chase

stop beside her. She was exhausted, but the minute he stepped up next to her, her body ignited. *Oh shit.* She had to get this under control. Everyone around them would be able to smell her lust. Chase growled low in his throat, and she felt a shiver run down her spine.

"Knock it off, Chase," Angel muttered, resisting the sudden urge to step closer to him. "Just stop. I can't do this right now."

"I'm not doing anything, Baby," he growled, his voice low and sexy as hell. "But if you don't control your own hormones, I will be doing you in the back of that fucking SUV."

Angel closed her eyes and took a deep breath, trying to calm down. This could not be happening right now. She knew who Chase was to her, but she just couldn't deal with it. She did not want a mate. Not now. Not ever. She had too many personal problems, too many ghosts, too many enemies. She didn't wish that on anyone. Taking the coward's way out, she moved toward Nico and said, "Hey, Nico, I'm heading out. I need to get some sleep. We will all meet back here tomorrow at 10 a.m. to discuss our next step."

Glancing back at Chase, she told him, "I will meet with you at 9:30 to give you a rundown on what happened on the op." Not waiting for a reply, she turned and hopped into the SUV, her team all piling in behind her. She had to get out of there, and fast.

Nico pulled back from Jenna, and looked over at Chase. "Angel said you will have someone guarding us at all times. The General is still out there. Until he is caught, I want twenty-four-hour surveillance on Jenna and Lily. And I want the best."

Chase nodded his eyes following the SUV as it left the compound. "When Angel called earlier, I contacted the council and told them the situation. They are sending Storm and Ryker back down. They should be here within a couple of hours. Until then, Bran and my head enforcer, Slade, will be right outside your door."

"I want Aiden and Xavier, too," Nico said. Chase looked at him in surprise. "They screwed up once, they won't do it again," Nico told him. "I want them."

"Then you will have them," Chase agreed, knowing what Nico said was true. The enforcers were upset with themselves, and would do everything in their power to make up for their mistake. Walking over to Jenna and Lily, he gave them both a gentle hug. "Hey, honey, I am so glad you're home," he whispered to his niece. "So glad."

Lily looked up at him solemnly. "It's okay, Uncle Chase. I'm safe now. Daddy and Angel killed the bad guys."

With tears in his eyes, Chase gave her a tight hug and whispered, "Yes, Honey, it is going to be just fine now. You are going to be safe." He would make damn sure of it. No one messed with his family and got away with it. And it didn't look like his tough-as-nails mate was going to just let it slide either. Chase gave Lily a soft kiss, before turning to head back into the building to his office. He needed to speak to Aiden and Xavier to let them know that they were being added to Jenna and Lily's security detail. They were good enforcers. Nico was right, they would not fuck up again, because if they did, they would answer to him.

13

Nico followed Jenna to her home, his gaze straying
to her ass as she walked. Check the fence, check
the buildings, check the grounds, check Jenna's ass. Now
that Lily was home and safe inside the compound, all he
could think about was taking his mate and marking her as
his for everyone to see. When she glanced back at him and
caught his eyes straying down once again, her eyes heated
up. "We need to get Lily fed, bathed, and in bed first," she
said quietly. Nico nodded, his gaze hot on hers.

They moved up the sidewalk of a small cottage-style
house that was light green in color with white trim. "A lot
of the pack live in apartments in the buildings by the
offices," Jenna said, "but I wanted a real home for Lily. We
plant flowers in the window sills and around the house
together. She really enjoys it. It's a little cold this April
still, so we were going to start planting them in May."

"And Momma mows the grass," Lily said, as she
opened her mouth wide in a yawn. Even though she had
slept quite a bit, she was still worn out from the trauma

she had gone through. "I'm not big enough yet, but someday I will be."

As they entered the house, Nico had them wait by the front door so he could do a sweep of the area. When he was sure it was safe, he told Jenna to give Lily a bath and he fixed her something to eat. In the kitchen, he cooked up some hamburger meat and mixed it with a box of macaroni and cheese he found in the cupboard, adding some Velveeta to make it creamier. When Jenna came into the kitchen with a warm, clean Lily, it was obvious the little girl was not going to be able to stay awake much longer.

Nico sat down on a chair and reached his arms out to Lily, smiling when she immediately came to him. He held her while she ate her dinner, just snuggling her close and breathing in her clean, fresh scent. When she was done, Nico stood with her in his arms, and then followed Jenna to Lily's room. He gently placed the child on her bed, covering her up with her soft pink blankets.

Lily snuggled Shadow and her blanky close and looked up at Nico. "Promise you will be here when I wake up," she demanded.

"You better believe it, princess," he replied, running a hand gently down her hair. "I will be right here waiting for you." As she clutched his hand, scared to let go, he started to sing to her. He had a beautiful voice, and with a soft sigh, she was soon sound asleep.

Jenna bent down and kissed Lily on the cheek, and then she glanced over at him. Nico wanted her, and he was done waiting. Standing, he followed Jenna out of the room and down the hall to her bedroom, shutting the door behind them.

"I need to know, Jenna," he said, as he stood in front of her, his hands clenched tightly into fists, "Are you all right with this after what happened? Are you scared? I would never hurt you."

Jenna closed the distance between them and placed a hand on his chest, looking up into his eyes. "I want this, Nico. I want you. I haven't been with anyone since that night, but I want to be with you. You're different. I feel safe with you."

Reaching out, he gently trailed the back of his hand down her cheek. "I will never hurt you, Jenna. Never. You are my mate. Mates are meant to be cherished and cared for above all else. Never hurt."

Slowly, he lowered his head and skimmed her lips with his. Once, twice, and then he traced them with his tongue. A low growl ripped from his throat and he gripped her by her hips, swinging her around and shoving her up against the wall. "I want to go slow with you, Jenna. I want to, but I don't know if I can. I need you now." As he thrust his tongue into her mouth again and again, he ground his hard length into her.

"Oh God," she cried out. "Don't stop, Nico. I don't need slow. Fuck me, now."

Nico lost it. He ripped her shirt from her and sliced open her bra with a claw. Panting, he looked at her breasts, his eyes going full wolf. "Mine," he growled. "Mine!" Her pants were shredded from her body and his quickly followed.

"Off," she demanded, tearing at his shirt. Nico yanked it up and over his head and then grabbed her, picking her back up and shoving her against the wall. As his mouth closed around one of her nipples, sucking it deeply, she cried out and rubbed herself up and down his length. She was so hot, so wet. And it was all for him.

Nico leaned back and looked into Jenna's eyes as he held her hips tightly and he shoved deep inside her. Her eyes closed, and she let out a deep moan of pleasure as she slammed her head back against the wall. Nico moved inside her, groaning loudly as he rocked his hips harder and faster. Then, as he felt her body clench around him, he buried his teeth deeply into her shoulder, marking her as his, and let himself come inside of her. He felt the sharp sting of her fangs and then pure bliss as she returned his bite on his shoulder.

Breathing heavily, low growls of satisfaction vibrating in his chest, Nico slowly lowered Jenna to the floor as he licked at the mate bite, healing it. He shivered as he felt Jenna doing the same. After a moment, he picked her up and carried her to the bathroom. Giving her a soft kiss, he let her feet slide to the ground and moved over to turn on the shower. He would clean them, and then they would get some rest. They still had a long ways to go to end this nightmare they had been pulled into, and as much as Nico wanted to forget about everything but Jenna, he had a duty as her mate to keep both her and Lily safe.

14

As soon as they reached Angel's house, the team split up, and went to their own homes. They needed sleep, and Angel needed her space.

Making her way to the back bedroom, she opened the huge safe hidden in the back of the closet, quickly storing her gear, except for the Glock that she always kept on her. Once she was done, she headed toward the kitchen.

Opening the fridge, she grabbed a bottle of wine that she had opened the day before but had never had any of, and then got a wine glass from the cupboard. Sometimes she just sipped from the bottle, but she could be classy when she wanted to.

As she walked into her bedroom, Angel laid her gun on the nightstand, and then stripped on her way to the bathroom, leaving a trail of clothes behind her. Whatever, she would get them later. Right now, what she really needed was a nice long bubble bath. She loved the large, deep tub in her bathroom. It was one of the reasons she had bought the house years ago. She had always wanted one so that she could light candles around it, have some wine, and relax, forgetting about the rest of the world. And after a long mission, nothing was better.

Angel started the water, making it as hot as she could stand it. She added some bubbles, then went over and turned on the radio that was on the small hutch across the room. Country music soothed her, too. She loved it. None of that boring classical crap for her, although she did enjoy some hard rock at times, too.

There were candles set around the bathroom. Angel lit them all and shut off the lights. Swiftly, she pinned her long, blonde hair up into a messy bun, and then stepped into the tub. She let out a low moan as she slid into the hot, steamy water. It felt so damn good.

Angel shut off the water and leaned back, closing her eyes. Immediately her thoughts went to Chase. No, hell no. She tried to think of something else, anything else, but it didn't work. Even after draining the bottle of wine, she could only think of Chase. Finally, Angel gave up and got out of the tub. So much for relaxing.

Two hours later, she was still wide awake. She had been in bed for two fucking hours, and no matter what she did, she still could not sleep. Part of the reason was because of the huge adrenaline rush they'd all had when they went in after Lily. Part was the fact that it was 3:00 in the afternoon and the sun was high in the sky. But most of it was the hot, sexy alpha that was only forty minutes away. Her body was on fire just thinking about him. Well, she thought, she might not be able to be with him, but she could at least take care of one of her issues so she could sleep right now.

Angel pulled her shirt up over her head, and then

slipped her shorts down her legs and off. Slowly, she trailed her fingers from her neck down over one breast. Cupping it, she gently pinched the hard nipple, and a moan escaped her. She breathed out Chase's name as she imagined it was his hands on her body, gliding over her skin. He was so sexy, with his gorgeous blue eyes and deeply tanned skin. Just the thought of him made her hot as hell. As she stroked her breasts, in her mind she was running her hands over the hard muscles of his chest. She slowly moved one of her own hands down lower and touched her sensitive clit. Her hips jumped up as she almost came just from that. *Oh God, Chase, please*, she moaned in her mind, mentally moving her hands down his chest and cupping his rock-hard cock. She stroked him harder and faster in her mind as she matched the rhythm to the fingers stroking herself. Suddenly, she shouted as she exploded, and she heard him roar when he came on his end.

As she drifted off to sleep, in her mind she saw Chase's clear, blue eyes dark with passion and heard him snarl, *Mine. Mine.*

"Fuck," Chase growled, as he stripped his jeans off and moved into the private bathroom in his office. He had been at the end of a meeting with the council enforcers when he felt the first stirring in his mind. He hadn't been sure what was happening, until he somehow heard Angel's thoughts and caught his name on a moan coming out of her mouth.

He had watched as she stroked her beautiful golden

breasts down to her clit and had just about come in his damn jeans before he had finally gotten Storm and Ryker out the door. He had torn open his jeans and then felt her hands on his rock-hard, straining cock. As she had stroked him harder and faster, in his mind he had watched her long fingers moving faster on her clit. When she squeezed her nipple, Chase had lost it. He had grabbed himself and stroked hard and fast a few times before shooting all over the place as he heard her coming. *Mine,* he had growled. *Mine.* Angel might not want to admit it for some reason, but she was his. His mate, the other half of his soul, and he would have her.

15

Nico woke up to the feeling of sweet, soft woman in his arms. He breathed in their combined scents and let out a sigh of contentment. When a couple mated, combining blood and sex, their scents became one and let everyone else know they were taken. Now everyone would know Jenna was his. Supreme satisfaction flowed through him.

He noticed the alarm clock said it was only 2 a.m., and wondered what had woken him up. Kissing Jenna gently on her brow, he untangled himself from his mate and slipped out of bed. Grabbing his pants off the floor and yanking them on, he palmed his Glock off the nightstand and silently made his way out into the hall.

Crouching low to the floor, Nico moved quietly toward the kitchen where he could hear noises. Going slowly just in case it was Lily, he stopped against the wall and peered around the doorway. His eyes met a pair of dark green ones, and he shook his head as he watched Phoenix take a big swallow of diet coke from where he sat at the kitchen table. "Ya know, your mate really needs to get some of the loaded shit in here. Or better yet, some beer. This tastes like crap."

"What in the hell are you doing here, Phoenix?" Nico grumbled, thumbing the safety on the Glock and shoving it in the back of his pants. Pulling out a chair with his foot, he straddled it and faced Phoenix with his arms over the back of it.

"The condo was lonely without your ugly mug," Phoenix replied with a shrug.

Nico looked at him carefully, one eyebrow raised. "No man, what are you really doing here?

"Guarding your happy ass because obviously no one else can do it," Phoenix stated, shaking his head in disgust. "Do you know how easy it was to sneak in here? First off, it was child's play to get over the fence. And, tell me, how many enforcers are watching this place? I counted six, and that's including the council enforcers. Granted, they were a little bit harder to maneuver around, but I did it. I'm sorry, Nico, but that's fucked up. This is your mate and child we are talking about. I made it in here, so someone else can, too. We need to keep them safe, my brother."

"There aren't many as good as you, Phoenix, but I get what you're saying. Crash in the living room the rest of the night? Help me protect my family?"

"You got it," Phoenix nodded. That was it. That was all that needed to be said. Nico got up and walked out, heading toward Lily's room to check on her, while Phoenix leaned back in his chair and finished his soda.

Nico stopped in Lily's doorway and just watched her for a moment. Then, he silently moved over by her bed and asked softly, "What's wrong, Princess?"

Lily looked up at him with tear-filled eyes. "I'm scared," she whispered.

Nico reached down and picked her up, scooping up her blanket and Shadow, too. Kissing her softly on the forehead, he moved toward Jenna's room. "You never have to be alone when you are scared, honey. Your mommy and I are right here."

Jenna woke up as he entered the room and scooted over in the bed when she saw them. Leaning down, Nico placed Lily beside her, pulling the covers up over them. "Where are you going?" Jenna asked as Nico picked up his shirt and moved toward the door.

"Just out for a bit. I want to check on things. You two rest, and I'll be back soon."

───────

As Nico made his way past the living room again, he saw Phoenix in the recliner, kicked back like he was taking a nap with a baseball cap over his face. Looks were deceiving though, because Nico knew that by now Phoenix would be tuned in to every little noise in the house, and if anyone tried to come in, it would be the last stupid thing they ever did.

"I'm going out back," Nico said, and saw Phoenix nod once. Walking out the back door, he made his way over to the swing set. Putting his hand on the slide, he stood silently and waited. He did not have to wait long.

"Did Phoenix make it inside okay?" Storm asked softly as she appeared by his side. Nico chuckled, shaking his head in amusement. "Yeah, he did. Anyone else see him?"

"Nope. He snuck in on this side and Ryker was at the

front of the house. I recognized him, so figured you wouldn't mind if I let him go. Didn't want to raise a fuss and risk waking everyone in the house up."

"Thanks, Storm," Nico said, bumping her shoulder with his own. "Nice to know at least one of you isn't sleeping on the job."

A slow grin tipped up the corners of her mouth and she motioned to the house. "Go in to your mate and child, Nico. Ryker and I got this. And obviously you have Phoenix on the inside. Enjoy the few hours you can right now."

Nico thanked her, smiling as he made his way back into the house. Storm was good at her job. His family was going to be just fine with her there. Crossing over to where Phoenix was sprawled out, he laughed quietly as he said, "Guess you didn't quite make it like you thought. Storm made ya, buddy."

Phoenix pushed his hat up off his eyes and a self-satisfied grin appeared on his face. "Good for her. But then, all the girls notice me, don't they?" he joked.

Nico grinned, "You always were a cocky son of a bitch. Get some rest. I'll see you in the morning."

He teased Phoenix, but they both knew that even though he might act like it sometimes, he wasn't the type of person that was cocky or full of himself. Hell, he hadn't been laid in at least nine months. He was tired of fast women. He wanted to find someone that would love him for who he was, not just the dick in his pants. He wanted someone for himself like Nico had found in Jenna. A woman or mate that would love him unconditionally, scars and all.

Phoenix wasn't a shifter. Nope, he was all human, but

he was all badass human. He had grown up in foster homes and learned quickly that you either became the biggest, meanest, badass around, or you got the shit kicked out of you all of the time.

Well, he definitely wasn't a pussy. He had tangled with some pretty mean fuckers, both humans and shifters, and won. He had spent years in the military out in the jungle tracking and eliminating the enemy, but he was tired.

He wanted a chance to be himself for once. Yes, he was a big, bad mother, but he was also a deep, gentle soul. An artist who loved to draw and paint, and could see beauty in things most people couldn't.

Phoenix just wanted someone to really know him and to want the real him. That was why he hadn't had sex in over nine months. He was holding out for that one woman. He knew she was out there and he vowed to wait for her, no matter how long it took. No more fast hookups. No more one-night stands. He was going to find his one and only, his soul mate.

16

J enna rolled over in bed, sitting up quickly when she realized it was empty. Where were Nico and Lily? Closing her eyes, she listened intently, relief filling her when she heard voices in the kitchen area. They belonged to Nico and Lily, and there was one other voice that she didn't quite recognize. Nico and Lily were laughing at something the man was saying. A slow smile crossed Jenna's lips when she smelled bacon and pancakes. She couldn't remember the last time she'd eaten, and a giggle slipped free when her stomach began to growl.

Throwing back the covers, Jenna jumped out of bed and dressed quickly. Then she headed toward the kitchen to see what was so funny. As she pushed open the door, she saw a tall man with very broad shoulders facing the stove. His head was shaved, and a tattoo of some kind of tribal design ran up the nape of his neck. When he turned to look at her, she saw another tattoo peeking out of the top of his tee shirt. He was wearing her pink frilly apron and she couldn't help grinning at him. He looked like such a big mean bastard, but then he was in pink.

He winked at her and flipped the pancake up in the air, catching it in the frying pan on the way back down. Lily giggled again. "That one is mine, Mommy," she said, her eyes alight with excitement. "Phoenix is making it look like a rabbit for me."

"A rabbit?" Jenna asked.

"Of course, all wolves eat rabbits!" Lily said. At that, peals of laughter flowed throughout the room.

Jenna picked Lily up in her arms and swung her around, making her giggle even harder. Then she sat down with Lily on her lap and leaned into Nico, giving him a soft kiss and rubbing her cheek against his.

Of course, she knew who Phoenix was now. He was a member of Angel's team. She had been under so much stress before that she doubted she would be able to recognize and name the whole team.

"When did you get here, Phoenix?" she asked. She did not remember hearing the doorbell ring that morning. But then, she had been so out of it, she hadn't even heard Nico and Lily get up.

"I slept in the chair in the living room, Ma'am," he said politely.

Wow, she thought. This man was definitely not the man you would think he was at first glance. "In the chair?" She asked him in confusion.

"Phoenix showed up late last night," Nico told her. "He and I live together in the city. Big guy was lonely without me. I wasn't there to watch Lifetime with him."

Phoenix actually blushed, "Hey, they have good shows on sometimes!"

"Mommy watches Lifetime," Lily piped up, clapping her hands together in delight when Nico and Phoenix burst into laughter.

Jenna watched Phoenix as he turned around and made Lily's plate for her. "Thank you for protecting us," she said softly. He glanced back at her and nodded once with a smile, then he handed Lily her plate and started to make another one.

The man was full of contradictions, Jenna thought. A big badass full of tattoos that liked to cook, helped his friend protect his family, and blushed when being teased about watching Lifetime. And let's not forget that he looked pretty in pink, she thought with a giggle.

"Stop checking out my brother," Nico growled playfully. Jenna just laughed at him. She was his now. The bite on her shoulder proved it. She would never stray and would never leave Nico, just as he would never do anything like that to her. Mates did not cheat, and they could not stand to be apart for any length of time.

"Well, tonight you will stay in the guest room," she stated, accepting the plate he handed her.

He smiled, his eyes warm with gratitude as he said, "Thanks, ma'am."

17

A ngel pulled up in front of the little cottage and parked. She and the rest of the team jumped out and walked up the sidewalk, scanning the area on the way. They knew exactly where every enforcer was and where the weak points in their protection detail were by the time they made it to the door. It was not that the way the enforcers had things set up was wrong necessarily, but it was not the way RARE would have done it. They obviously had not had the same training as the team. There were weak areas that RARE would not have had.

The door opened when they reached it, with Phoenix on the other side. "Chase swapped his enforcers out with fresh ones at 6 a.m.," he told them, "but the council enforcers are still out there. They haven't taken a break since they showed up yesterday."

"Go tell them to get some rest. You guys can stay with Nico and his family while I meet with Chase, then I will come back here for our meeting," Angel told him. "Tell them to be here later this afternoon after they've had some sleep. We will be around until at least 6 p.m."

When Phoenix left to deliver her orders, Angel stepped into the house. The only warning she got was a loud squeal before Lily came running and threw herself at Angel. When she picked her up, Lily latched her arms around Angel's neck in a tight hold. "You're leaving again tonight," she whispered against her neck. "You, and Daddy, and Phoenix."

Angel held her tightly as she replied, "I wasn't planning on leaving for a couple of days, Sweetheart."

Lily shook her head. "No, it has to be tonight. If you don't go tonight, they will all die."

Everyone froze as Lily's words reached them. "Who will die, Lily?" Nico asked, coming up behind her.

"The mommies and kids," Lily said. "It's going to blow up and everyone is going to die."

Angel looked at Jenna and growled, "Get Chase here now."

Phoenix, get your ass in here now, Lily said we have to leave tonight. She said if we don't, a lot of people are going to die. Tell Ryker and Storm to get some rest, but to be back here by 1pm. We need them to watch Jenna and Lily while we are gone.

After sending the message to Phoenix, Angel sat on the couch, cuddling Lily closer as she said, "Lily, I need to see what you are talking about, all right? I promise, it won't hurt. Just close your eyes while I take a peek inside your mind and see." Phoenix burst through the door, and then all of Angel's team surrounded her as she made herself vulnerable, connecting with Lily.

When Angel merged her mind with Lily's, she told her gently, *I need you to show me what you saw.* Immediately,

Lily pulled up the vision so Angel could follow along. They were in what looked like some kind of a huge warehouse building. There were cages on one wall and rooms with windows on another. Angel saw a little bear cub in one cage, and two others had wolf pups in them. In one of the rooms was an extremely pregnant woman sitting on a bed with her head bowed. She was rubbing her stomach, and it looked like she was singing.

Another room held a woman with long red hair. She was pregnant, but didn't look as far along as the first woman. And she was pissed off. She was yelling at the guards on the other side of a window, who in turn were laughing at her. Suddenly, her eyes seemed to widen in surprise as she stared straight back at Angel. She immediately schooled her expression and kept yelling. Angel tuned into what she was saying and heard, "You are nothing but a bunch of dickless cowards. You think you can keep us in this godforsaken place and breed us, then steal our babies and hurt them? Fuck you all! You don't think anyone is looking for us? You don't think they will look here in Mexico? We are in freaking Tijuana, you stupid fucks. Someone is going to find us! And when they do, I will make you all pay for what you have done to us! I will gut you like the spineless bastards you are!" She looked one more time in Angel's direction, then turned away and muttered, "Seriously, hiding us right in the middle of Tijuana. If I could just get out of this building, I could get help. There are so many tourists around this place, someone would help me. My God, we are right by the freaking market place."

After that, the vision moved on quickly, showing the guards drinking and laughing. Two guards went in after the red-haired woman, grabbing her and forcing themselves on her, then there was a huge boom and the place just blew apart.

Everyone was caught in the blast and killed; the cub, the pups, the women and the guards. Angel was not going to let that happen. No way in hell. That last woman with the fiery red hair...she couldn't let her die. She had to come home. Her mate was waiting for her.

Nico was watching Angel closely, and immediately knew when she slipped out of Lily's mind and became aware of her surroundings again. Chase had arrived while she was in the vision with Lily, and as soon as the team moved back away from her, he went and knelt down in front, of her placing a hand on her cheek. Angel closed her eyes, and Nico was shocked when she leaned into his touch for a moment. He had never seen her do anything like that before. Not even with her teammates, and she considered them family.

Angel seemed to get control of herself and she pulled away from Chase. She looked over at Lily, and reaching out, she wiped the tears away that were falling down her face. "Thank you, Lily. Thank you for showing me what you saw. Now, you go with your mama and play out on your swing set while I talk to everyone."

Nico stepped forward and gathered Lily into his arms, giving her a hug before handing her over to Jenna. "Go play, Princess. I will see you in a little bit."

As they left, Nico moved back in the room and sat down on the couch by Angel, Chase sitting on the other side of her. The rest of the team gathered around and waited for her to speak.

"Chase, you need to get Bran here now. I will start once he arrives, but he needs to get here now, and he needs to be involved in everything regarding this rescue mission." Surprisingly, Chase didn't ask questions. He just grabbed his phone and placed the call.

"What are you going to tell him, boss?" Nico asked quietly.

Angel's eyes met his, and she said, "Everything. He needs to know."

When Bran arrived just a few minutes later, Angel motioned for him take a seat in the chair across from her. She explained everything that had happened with Lily's kidnapping to him, including the team's and Lily's psychic abilities. He looked at Chase once she was done and asked, "Is this the truth?" Chase gave him a nod, and that was all it took. Bran had complete confidence in his alpha. If he said it was true, then it was.

"He is breeding the women," Angel said, glancing around the room at each of them. "I am positive it's the General, and he is trying to match psychic men and women with shifters. There is a bear cub, two wolf pups, and two pregnant women. One is very pregnant; the other is not as far along." Angel paused for a moment. "We need to get them all out of there, but we really need to get the second woman out now." She glanced around at all of them again, pausing on each one individually. "We are not going in alone this time, guys." Nico watched her for a moment as she seemed to gather her thoughts. Looking over at Chase she said, "I need Ryker, Storm, Aiden, Xavier, and Slade on guard duty for Jenna and Lily until we get back. I need Bran to come with us."

"Why me?" Bran asked in confusion.

Angel looked over at him, reaching out to lay a hand on his as she said, "One of the pregnant women is a feisty red head. She wasn't very far along, maybe four or five months. She seemed to notice me as I watched the vision unfold and she told me where they were. If we don't get there soon, she is going to be raped by two of the guards right before the building explodes. Bran, she is your mate."

"What the fuck," Bran roared, surging to his feet. "Are you messing with me?" Angel shook her head. "No, now sit your ass down and listen to me."

Chase got up and put his hand on Bran's shoulder, growling low in his throat and pushing some of his alpha power his way to get Bran to calm down. "Listen to Angel, Bran. She is risking a lot by allowing you to go along this time. She never takes anyone because it could easily screw up her mission. I have no clue why she's taking you, but you better calm the hell down and listen to her so she doesn't change her mind."

Bran slowly got control of himself, but it took a few minutes. To find out he had a mate, one that was being held by sadistic bastards and was possibly going to be raped by them, if she had not already been, was killing him. God, she was pregnant, so that meant she probably had been violated already. He was going to kill every last mother fucker in that place. He looked up at Angel. "I have no idea why you are letting me go, but let's get the hell out of here. I need to get to my mate."

"Flame," Angel said gently. "Your mate's name is Flame."

Bran took in a deep breath and closed his eyes, nodding. "And I am letting you go because she will die if I don't."

19

While Jaxson made the phone call to have the jet fueled and ready for them, Nico went outside to talk to Jenna and Lily. Lily looked over as he approached and smiled, her dimples showing. "Catch me, Daddy!" she squealed as she took off down the slide. Laughing, he ran over and scooped her up, throwing her in the air. As he hugged her again, she placed a hand on his cheek and smiled. "Don't worry, Mama and I will be okay."

Nico smiled at her and said, "Yes, you will. And I promise I will be home just as soon as I can."

He turned as he heard Storm's voice. "Hey there, Lily. Let's see which one of us can swing higher!"

"I thought you were resting," Nico said.

"I'll rest when I'm dead," she quipped back.

"That's our motto," he said, laughing. "You should really leave the council and come to work with us."

Storm just laughed. "I don't know if I could put up with all of that testosterone in one place."

Nico laughed, and then grabbed Jenna's hand and

pulled her back toward the house. When they walked in, the team was still in the living room debating on the best way to launch the rescue. As they walked by, Angel stopped them. "Congratulations on your mating."

"We will have a mating ceremony as soon as possible," Chase promised them. Basically, that meant they were going to have one kick ass party. Nico and Jenna were already mated, but at the ceremony, Chase would announce it to the pack, approve it, and everyone would party until dawn.

"We leave in twenty minutes, Nico," Angel said. "Move this outside by the car," she told the rest of them. "Let's let them say goodbye in peace."

"Bow chica bowwow," Rikki drawled.

Everyone laughed as they moved out the front door. "I really don't want to think about my sister like that," Chase groused.

They heard the door shut as they hit the bedroom. Nico had Jenna stripped in record time and soon he was sliding into her warm, wet heat balls deep. "God," he growled into her ear. "I don't want to leave you." He pounded into her desperately as she clung to him. It wasn't long before Nico felt her clench tightly around him and he let himself come at the same time she did, latching onto her shoulder with his teeth, claiming her once again. She cried out as she sank her own fangs in deep.

After a few moments, Nico lifted his head and gazed down at her. "You are so beautiful," he whispered. "I wish I could stay here and make love to you the rest of the day."

Jenna smiled softly at him as she reached up and slid her fingers through his short dark hair. "Me, too, but your team needs you. I will be here waiting for you when you come home."

Nico kissed her one more time before he got up and went into the bathroom to wash up quickly. When he came back out, Jenna was waiting for him. Closing the distance between them, she reached up and placed a chain around his neck. At the end of it was a small medallion that had a carving of two wolves with two small wolf pups in the background. "This was my father's," Jenna told him. "When I was younger, he told me that one day I was to give this to my own mate for good luck. I want you to take it with you now. I will pray that it helps bring you back to me."

Nico pulled her close, nuzzling his chin on her head. "I will come home to you," he promised. After a few minutes, he kissed her again, and then got dressed and they moved downstairs. He kissed her one last time before walking out the door to his waiting team. When they loaded up in the SUV to leave, he glanced back at his mate and smiled, saluting her with a cocky grin as they drove off. She laughed, shaking her head, and saluted him back.

20

The team stopped at their homes and geared up before heading to the airport. Bran was going crazy waiting, but the team had to be prepared for anything. They never went on a mission without an overload in gear and a plan of attack. Never. If you did not plan and prepare, then mistakes were made. Mistakes meant death, and Angel refused to allow anything to happen to her team.

They were at the airport and in the air flying to a little airstrip that didn't even show up on a map within an hour. They went over the plan again and again on the way there. They needed it to be flawless if they were to get into Mexico and get back out without any casualties.

Angel would try to connect with Flame once they got to the market area. She had connected with her just briefly in the vision, so she thought she would be able to do it again. Once they figured out what warehouse the women and children were being held in, they would fan out around the building and do some quick recon. Trace and Rikki would find places to hole up with their sniper rifles.

The team would come in from different areas if possible and spread out until they found out what part of the building everyone was being held in.

Bran's main focus was to be on rescuing his mate. He would not be able to talk to the rest of the team telepathically, but thanks to Jaxson, they all sported some techy communication devices to fix that small problem.

Jaxson was to try and find any computers that might have useful data on them regarding whatever the breeding program was and download it.

The rest of the team was to focus on kicking ass and taking names, and on getting everyone else out of that building before it blew. Because it would blow. Phoenix would make sure of that. To take down the monster, they would destroy every tentacle of his they could find. He wouldn't be able to hide indefinitely. They would find him. Then he would die.

21

Once again, darkness was their friend. The team swarmed silently through the market area keeping in the shadows. The nightlife in Tijuana was going strong, and Angel and her team did not want to be spotted. They wanted to get in and out without drawing attention to themselves.

It was a huge risk taking Bran in with them this time, but he was following Angel's instructions, so she was letting it slide. They needed him if Flame was going to make it home alive.

Angel crept behind a building, becoming one with the shadows surrounding it. She stopped beside it and spoke very softly, "I'm going to try and connect with Flame now." Nico came up beside her to guard her and keep her safe. Bran was on the other side. Normally it would have been Phoenix, but if Chase trusted Bran enough to make him his beta, then she would trust him, too. Because even though she was not ever going to act on it, she knew that

Chase was her mate. And above all else, a mate protected what was his.

Silently, she closed her eyes and concentrated on the fiery, red haired woman that she had seen in the vision before. It didn't take long before she saw that Flame was sitting in a corner on the floor, hugging her legs up to her chest. As Angel connected with her, she felt the dark pain ripping through Flame's stomach. She knew immediately what was happening. Flame was losing the baby. It was happening fast, and it was very painful, but Flame was not saying a word.

FLAME PANTED SOFTLY, her head bowed on her knees, with her hands clenched tightly together. She knew there was nothing that could be done to help her baby, he was already gone. And she was afraid to bring attention to herself.

The guards were in a rowdy mood tonight. The last time they were like this, she had watched helplessly as they raped the woman in the room next to her. The woman had screamed and cried as they took turns with her, begging them to stop, but there was nothing Flame could do to help. She had tried. The guards had brought her into the same room and made her watch. They'd tied her to a chair, her arms secured behind her back and her legs tied to the legs of the chair. Flame had fought and fought to get free and get to the other woman, but no matter how hard she had tried, she couldn't. She had yelled at them, had threatened them, but they just laughed. They had told her that her time was coming, and they wanted her to see how good it was going to be.

The woman had cried for her baby. Had held her stomach and begged them not to hurt her baby. But they just laughed at her, too. They told her that the brat would be fine, that you could not hurt a baby from having sex. By the time they were done with the woman, she was pretty much comatose. She just laid there in shock. They did not even bother to clean her up. Flame hadn't heard her utter a word since then, except for singing to her baby. She could feel how much pain the other woman was in, how terrified she was, but there wasn't a damn thing she could do to help her.

Right now, Flame kept quiet and suffered in silence. She knew she was losing her baby. She knew he was already dead. And if she called out to the guards for help, she was afraid that they would come in and use her like they had the other woman. Afraid they would see that there was no way she could protect herself from them now. They were all such twisted fucks. You never knew what they were thinking. It would not matter to them that she was in the middle of losing a child, they would just wait until it was done and then take their turns with her while she was helpless. It was not like there was a doctor there anyway, only the scientists. And she didn't want any of them anywhere near her, either.

Flame froze when she felt another's presence in her mind. It was familiar, but not. *Who are you?* she whispered. She had felt that same presence touch her mind a few hours ago. It had just touched briefly, but Flame recognized it. It was the woman she had seen when she was yelling at the guards earlier, with long blonde hair and blue eyes. She'd prayed that the woman had listened to her when she threw out the hints as to where they were being held. That she would help her somehow.

We are coming for you, Flame, the woman whispered in her mind. *We are here. We are in Tijuana, in the market place. I don't know what building you are in, though.*

Tears flowed down Flame's cheeks as she listened to the voice. She had prayed and prayed for months that someone would come after her. She had begun to lose hope. The guards hadn't broken her spirit yet, but they had come damn close.

She had thought she had left the worst of it behind when the General moved her to this location, away from Gideon after he had finally been able to get her pregnant. But she was wrong. At least with Gideon he was the only one raping her. Here, if the guards got ahold of her, it would be several of them at once.

Flame panted softly as another pain ripped through her belly. *Why don't you ask someone for help?* the woman asked.

There aren't any doctors here, Flame panted. *And the guards would rather fuck me than help me.*

Flame felt a hand stroke gently down her hair. It was a soothing gesture, one she hadn't felt in so long. *We are here now, Flame*, the voice said. *You aren't alone anymore. We are going to get you out.*

Who are you? Flame asked again.

My name is Angel, the voice said.

Angel, Flame whispered. *I could use an Angel right now.*

Angel chuckled softly. *I'm not your typical Angel, honey. You won't see any white wings on me, and definitely no halo. But you could think of me as The Angel of Death because I will be bringing death and destruction to everybody in that building that hurt you.*

Just my kind of Angel, Flame said. Flame heard Angel laugh as another pain slammed into her.

They're getting closer, Angel said.

Yes, Flame groaned. *Anytime now...He's already gone, Angel. I can feel it. My baby is already gone and there is nothing I can do about it.*

I know, hon, Angel responded. *We are gonna take that sweet baby home with us and we are going to give him a good burial, okay? And he is going to have those beautiful white angel wings that I don't have.*

Flame cried softly at that. *Thank you*, she whispered.

Do you have any idea where you are, Flame? Angel asked.

They thought I was drugged when they brought me here, Flame said, her brow furrowing as she tried to remember. *But most of it was already out of my system. I remember the building is red. A dark red. Another building by it had a sun on it. A bar or something. That's it, I'm sorry. That is all I saw.* Another pain ripped through Flame and she cried out softly. She was not going to be able to keep quiet much longer.

Flame looked up when she heard the door to her room open. A couple of guards were standing there grinning smugly at her. "By the blood all over the floor, I take it that thing inside of you is either dead, or about to be."

Oh God, Angel, hurry. Please hurry, Flame cried as the next wave of pain slammed into her and all hell broke loose.

22

Angel held onto the wall as she slowly opened her eyes. "Fuck," she ground out in anger. "She's here. She is right fucking here." Cursing again, she smacked the red wall she was leaning against, and then peered around the corner looking at the cantina next door with the bright yellow sun on it. Looking back at Nico and Bran, she snarled, "Flame saw a sun on the building next to the building she was taken to, and the building she is in is dark red in color. We have to get in there now. Flame is in the middle of losing the baby, and the guards just came into her room. She can't defend herself. Dammit, I wondered how I was able to keep the connection with her for so long. She is so close."

"Let's go!" Rikki said, slipping out of sight around the building, while Trace moved to a place just across the street, his rifle up, and his eyes trained on them.

"There is a door on the side by the cantina," Rikki told them quietly. "I'm in place. Let's rock and roll."

Bran jumped straight up, grabbing hold of a window sill on the second floor and pulled himself through the open window. "Well, that works," Nico said, before running around to the left side of the building as Phoenix went to the right and jumped in. Angel decided to use the front door. The thing was actually unlocked. They swept all of the floors quickly, but found no one.

"What the hell?" Bran snarled. "Where are they?"

Angel closed her eyes and silently slipped into Flame's mind again. The pain was excruciating. The baby had slipped out, but the guards were on her now. They were beating her. One had his pants undone, but was holding his junk and howling in pain. Way to go, Flame, Angel thought. The other one had her down and was digging his knee in her stomach. There was blood everywhere. Flame was so weak she could hardly move, but she turned her head and bit the guard as hard as she could on the wrist.

We are in the building, Flame. There isn't anyone here. How do we get to you? Angel yelled into Flame's mind.

She barely heard Flame's weak response. *Hidden door. Behind a bookcase. Goes down below.*

Angel felt Flame pass out as she came back to herself. She ran quickly to the room in the back of the warehouse where she had seen the bookcase, yelling at her team to follow. So much for making a quiet entrance. Those sick bastards were not raping Flame while she was passed out. "There's a door behind the bookcase. Hurry! They're hurting her!"

Bran let out a roar, and threw the bookcase across the room. Angel opened the door and the enraged man flew past her down the stairs. The first guard came at them from the bottom of the stairs. Bran snapped his neck before he could pull out his gun. "We got them, Bran! Get to Flame!" Angel cried.

As Bran kept moving, he heard a thump as a throwing star flew past his head and was imbedded in between the eyes of the next guard. He came up to a hallway and had to make a decision to go right or left. He took in a deep breath and smelled blood. Lots of blood. It was mixed with the scent of cinnamon and sunshine. Mate! He turned left and ran as hard as he could. There were gunshots and fighting all around him, but he didn't slow down until he came to the room that his Flame was in.

Bran bellowed loudly at the scene before him. Flame was on the floor, her eyes shut, her skin so pale, and surrounded in blood. One of the guards stood off to the side stroking his dick while the other guard had Flame's gown up around her thighs and was positioning himself between her legs. Her eyes snapped open at the sound, but Bran didn't hesitate. He grabbed a knife from his boot and let it fly. As it was embedded into the first guard's neck, Bran tackled the other one that was on top of Flame. They ended up on the other side of the room, Bran on top of the guard beating the hell out of him, seething with anger.

"Help me," he heard Flame beg softly, "please, help me." As the quiet pleas broke through the red haze in his mind, he scrambled off the guard and crawled over to Flame. The guard was dead, but his mate needed him.

There was so much blood, Bran wasn't sure what to do. "God, baby," he whispered, reaching down and softly stroking the hair back away from her face.

As tears squeezed out of her eyes, Flame weakly

pointed over to something on the floor by the wall. "Please, bring him with us. Please," she said weakly. Then she was out again.

Bran took a blanket off the bed and wrapped Flame up in it. Then he grabbed a sheet and wrapped it around the little boy. Placing the baby on his mother's stomach, he picked them both up and walked out of the room.

"Let's get the hell outta here before the building blows!" Bran heard Angel yell. He looked over to see that she was carrying one of the little wolf pups, Nico had the other one, and Jaxson held the bear cub close. Phoenix came out of the second room carrying a very pregnant woman who looked scared to death.

As he moved through the basement area, down the hall and up the stairs, Bran saw so much death. It did not affect him at all. They had all deserved to die. Anyone that touched and hurt what was his deserved to die. Guard or scientist- he didn't give a shit. And he would track down every last person that had a part in taking his mate and hand out the justice they deserved.

Bran ran out of the building with the rest of the team, and raced to the vehicle that would take them to the airfield. Trace tried to take the baby from him, but he refused. Flame was his mate, his responsibility. He would take care of her and her son. The building blew sky high when they were almost to the SUV. Ignoring the debris falling around them, they quickly piled into the vehicle and drove full throttle to the airstrip. They were in the air within minutes, flying hell bent out of Mexico.

"ANGEL, we gotta do something for Flame," Bran said quietly. "She's lost a lot of blood."

Angel nodded as she knelt down on the floor of the plane by where Bran had put Flame. "We are going to need to do a transfusion. We have some blood in the back. Nico will get it all set up."

"How did you know?" Bran asked in confusion.

Angel smiled at him. "Nico," was all she said.

Nico came over with a medical bag and set up an IV, putting it into Flame's arm and then hooking it up to a bag of blood he had. Then he hung the bag on a hook above their heads. As he started to undo the blanket around her body, Bran let out a low growl.

"I just need to check her, man. I need to make sure the bleeding has stopped," Nico told him, waiting for approval before lowering the blanket more. Bran let him, but he refused leave Flame's side. Angel handed him a clean gown, and once Nico confirmed the bleeding was under control, Bran changed her and wrapped her back up in a different blanket Angel passed to him. When he was done, Nico hooked another IV up with antibiotics in it.

Standing, Nico gently picked up the baby that was lying near Flame. "Where are you taking him?" Bran demanded, knowing Flame would be upset if she woke up and he was gone.

"Just to clean him up," Nico promised. "She is going to want to hold him, Bran, and I don't think she should see him like this."

Taking a deep breath, Bran nodded in agreement, and then sat down next to his mate. Unable to stop himself, he picked her up and held her on his lap. He wasn't surprised when she didn't stir. Leaning his head back, he finally let himself rest.

23

The plane bumped slightly as it hit the ground at the airport in Denver. Flame's eyes fluttered open and she stared up at the face of the man that held her. God, he was beautiful in sleep. Ash brown hair cut short, darkly tanned skin, gorgeous full lips. He had saved her, she remembered. He had busted into her room when the guard had her on the ground and was about to force himself on her, and he had saved her. And then he had called her baby.

She wanted to connect with him and see what he thought she was to him, but she was just too weak. And right now, it didn't really matter. She couldn't be his anything right now. Her life was so messed up; she couldn't be anything to anyone.

His eyes opened as she watched him. "Hi," he whispered.

"Hey," she whispered back.

He reached out and lightly ran his knuckle down the frown between her eyes. "Stop thinking so hard," he

RARE   95

said. "Right now is about taking care of you. Nothing
else."

Flame watched him for a moment, before slowly
nodding. Then she snuggled into him and closed her eyes,
losing consciousness again.

———————

BRAN STOOD UP, Flame in his arms, as Nico came over and
picked up her baby. Everyone filed off of the plane and
moved quickly toward the vehicles waiting for them. Bran
went straight to the SUV where his alpha stood, stopping
in front of him. Chase reached out a hand and grabbed his
shoulder and they stood in silence, Flame between them,
while Bran soaked up strength from his alpha.

After a moment, Chase opened the door and helped
Bran inside with his mate. Nico got in on the other side
with the baby, and Rikki climbed in back with Janie, the
pregnant woman that had been held with Flame.

Everyone else got into the other SUV with the children, Angel at the wheel. She followed Chase to the
compound and they pulled up in front of a building that
she hadn't been in yet. As she got out of the vehicle, she
saw Jenna run toward Nico, stopping abruptly when he
got out of the other SUV holding the baby. The smell of
death hung in the air and Jenna's eyes filled with tears.

Angel moved quickly to her side and quietly told her,
"Take Lily back home and I will send Nico there as soon
as I can."

Jenna turned around, gasping in surprise when she
saw that Lily had followed her and was standing there
staring in shock at the baby, too. "I thought she was with

Storm," she whispered. Gathering Lily up in her arms, Jenna whispered to Nico that she would see him soon, and moved quickly back toward the cottage.

When they entered the building, Angel realized it was a hospital for shifters. Shifters could not go to a regular hospital because they healed so much faster than humans, and their existence needed to remain a secret. Otherwise, they would have more than just the General to deal with.

A couple of nurses rushed over to where they stood and directed them all into different rooms. Nico followed Bran into the room he took Flame to. A nurse tried to take the baby from Nico, but Bran growled at her. She jumped back quickly and looked at the floor baring her neck in submission to the beta.

"It's okay," Flame said weakly. "I just want to hold him before you take him away, please. I haven't gotten to hold him yet."

The nurse's eyes jumped to Flame's in compassion. "Of course. If you would like me to, I could get him cleaned up for you first, while the doctor looks at you?"

"It's already been taken care of," Bran snapped. "Get the doctor in here now." The nurse nodded, her bottom lip trembling as she fought the urge to cry at the beta's fierce tone, and ran from the room.

Bran gently placed Flame on the bed and smoothed back her hair, placing a soft kiss on her forehead, then moving down to nuzzle her cheek. As he pulled back, the doctor rushed into the room. "Get out of my way, Bran," she demanded, glaring at him. "And stop scaring my nurses." Bran growled low in his throat, but backed away slightly so the doctor would have more room. She just rolled her eyes and moved up to the head of the bed by Flame.

"What's your name, Sweetheart?" she asked Flame softly. Flame watched her for a moment, her hands clenching the sheet she lay on tightly, before glancing over at Bran. The doctor had on a lab coat just like the scientists wore. She knew it was unreasonable, but it scared the hell out of her. Normally, she was as feisty as the next redhead, but right now she was weak, tired, and in so much pain. She would not be able to defend herself if anyone here tried to hurt her, and that scared the hell out of her.

"Bran," Flame whispered, fear pouring off her in waves.

He was around the bed and at her other side in an instant. Sitting down beside her on the bed, he gently pulled her into his arms and lightly stroked a hand down her hair. "It's okay, baby. I'm right here. No one is going to hurt you. I won't allow it. This is Dr. Josie Bennett. Doc Josie has been the pack doctor for years. I trust her."

Flame looked at the doctor in confusion. "But she looks so young," she whispered to Bran.

The doctor laughed, patting Flame lightly on the shoulder. "Shifters don't age like humans. I'm actually fifty-four years old. Bran here is one hundred and twenty-three."

Flames eyes grew wide in amazement. "You're not kidding?" she asked.

"Nope," the doctor said still laughing. "Your mate is an old man!"

Flame looked even more confused, "My what?" she asked.

Doc Josie's gaze flew from Flame to Bran. "Oh, I'm sorry! I thought you knew?"

"That's enough," Bran growled, interrupting the exchange. "Just check Flame out. She's human. She doesn't heal like us. She lost a lot of blood and needs to be looked at."

"Talk to me, Flame," the doctor said, all business now. "What am I looking for?"

A shudder ran through Flame as she looked over to where Nico held her son. "I lost my baby," she whispered.

"That's not all of it," Angel said from the doorway. "Some asshole had his knee shoved into her stomach pretty hard afterwards, too. And she's had no real medical attention since it happened. Just the basics to get her by until we could get her here to see a doctor, along with some pain medicine that should be wearing off soon."

Flame looked over at her and her eyes filled with tears. "You're still here," she whispered.

"You better believe it," Angel said, a small smile appearing. "I'm here, and I am not leaving until I know you're okay."

Flame returned her smile weakly, "You sure you don't have wings and a halo?" she asked.

Angel let out a harsh laugh, "Not even close, Sweetheart, not even close." Walking over to Nico, she took the baby from him and nodded to the door. "Go to your mate, Nico. She and Lily need you. I got this." As Nico left, Angel brought the baby over and put him in Flame's arms. The doctor began to protest, but Angel told her, "Nico looked her over on the plane and gave her an IV of antibiotics and some blood. Let her have a moment with her son." There was no give in Angel's voice, so the doctor sighed and backed off.

Tears streamed down Flame's face as she held her baby for what would be the first and last time. She slowly unwrapped the blanket and looked at him. He was so tiny. He had such little fingers and toes. Such tiny, perfect little ears. Flame cried and cried as she held him and gently stroked her fingers over his ears, nose, and arms. He was the size of her hand. So small and helpless. She vowed right then and there that she would hunt down everyone that was involved in what had happened to her and make them all pay. And Gideon, he would suffer the most.

24

W hen Nico reached the cottage, he heard the sweet sound of laughter coming from the back yard. Raking a hand through his hair, he stood for a moment soaking it in. The past few days had been hell. First with the mission they'd had rescuing the senator's son, then with Lily being kidnapped, and finally with the women and children they just rescued. He needed a break. He needed time to rest, but he also needed time to spend with Jenna and Lily. He wanted to get to know his sweet, beautiful mate better. He wanted to learn her likes and dislikes. Hell, he wanted to sit down and watch a movie with her, to just hold her.

And Lily. He had a daughter now. He had so many questions about her. Could she ride a bike yet? Or was that something he would get to teach her? Did she like to read? He would read a different story to her every night before bed if she wanted him to. What about her ABC's and numbers? He could help her with those. What about a pony? Did she want one? Hell, he would buy her a whole herd of ponies if it made her happy.

He knew they weren't safe from the General. That bastard was still out there, and he wanted Lily, but Nico was going to keep his family safe. And he knew Angel and the team would be there to help.

As he walked by some pink roses, Nico took out his knife and reached down to snip off two of them. After carefully removing the thorns, he walked around to the back of the house with them. His girls looked over as he rounded the corner, and Lily jumped off the swing and came running to meet him. Leaning down, he scooped her up, smacking a kiss loudly on her cheek and hugging her tightly.

"A rose for my princess," he said as he leaned back and handed her one of the roses.

She giggled, then whispered loudly, "You cut Mommy's roses, Daddy! You are gonna be in trouble!"

He laughed, snuggling her closer, loving that she called him Daddy. "We better not tell her where I got them from then, huh?"

As Jenna walked toward him, Nico felt his heart expand. Damn, he couldn't love her already. He had only known her for a few days. But, that was how it worked with mates. Once they sealed their souls together, there was nothing keeping them apart. He leaned down and kissed her softly, handing her the other pink rose. "A beautiful rose for a beautiful lady," he told her, nuzzling her ear. He breathed in deeply, taking in their shared scent. It was perfect.

"What should we do for the rest of the day, ladies?" he asked. "Anything you want, I'm all yours."

Jenna's smile grew as she leaned into him. "Really?" she whispered. "Doesn't Angel need you?"

"Not as much as my family needs me," Nico said, holding her close. "Angel sent me home to spend time with you. I will need to meet with everyone tomorrow to discuss security issues and other things, but today is for you and Lily."

"A picnic!" Lily squealed in delight. "Let's go on a picnic! And where's Phoenix? He needs to come, too!"

"Phoenix?" Nico said laughing. "I can hunt down Phoenix for you if you want."

Lily's eyes lit up, and she clapped her hands together in excitement. "Yes!"

They made their way into the house, and Jenna went to pack a picnic lunch while Nico placed a call to Phoenix. He found out that Phoenix was at the hospital still, helping out with the little bear cub. It seemed the cub had taken a liking to him and would not leave his side. He was still in bear form and refused to turn back to his human form. The doctor said it was a defense mechanism. The little boy was stronger in his bear form and felt like he needed to stay that way to protect himself. But, Phoenix said he would be over to go on the picnic soon. He would just bring the cub along.

When Phoenix and the cub arrived fifteen minutes later, their lunch was packed and ready. Heading out toward the beautiful land beyond all of the buildings in the compound, they walked for close to a mile before they came across the place Nico had seen in his vision. It was on the side of a hill, and there was a swing hanging from a tree, with another tree not too far away. Jenna walked over and spread a blanket out under the far tree, putting their picnic lunch on it. Yes, this was definitely his vision.

Nico nodded to Storm, Ryker, Aiden, and Xavier as they fanned out around them to keep watch. He was glad they had come with, even though Phoenix was there, too. He knew he wouldn't be able to keep guards on Jenna and Lily forever, but for now, he felt better with them there.

Lily smiled over at the bear cub, asking him if he would like to swing first. The cub watched her with wide brown eyes for a second, and then he glanced over at the swing. Turning to Phoenix, he crawled up his leg, digging his claws in. Phoenix grabbed him, pulling him all of the way up and snuggling him close. "It's okay, buddy," he said, running a hand over his fur.

"Hunter," Lily said softly. "His name is Hunter."

The bear cub swung his head around to Lily quickly, obviously surprised. She just smiled at him sweetly. "It's all right, Hunter. I will swing first, and when you are ready to shift so that you can have your turn, my mama brought you some clothes to put on." As Lily ran off to get on the swing, Hunter turned and nuzzled Phoenix under his chin, chuffing softly. "I gotcha, Hunter," Phoenix said quietly. "You're safe."

Nico pushed Lily on the swing, loving the sound of her laughter. She was so precious, he thought, as he pushed her higher. He glanced over at Jenna where she was sitting on the blanket watching them, a huge smile on her face. She was so damn beautiful.

Suddenly, the vision came out of nowhere, and he stood frozen as it played out in his mind. They were in the jungle and he stood at the top of a steep incline. He felt a searing pain in his chest. Looking down in horror, he watched as blood spread from the right side of his chest down. His team was yelling for him, but someone was dragging him away. It hurt so fucking bad, and he couldn't fight them off. "Oh yeah," he heard someone say, "he will be a perfect specimen for the program. The General will be pleased." Before his team could get to him, he was loaded onto a helicopter, and as it lifted into the air, he watched out of the window as Phoenix ran balls to the wall to catch him, screaming his name. Then he closed his eyes and the darkness came.

As Nico became aware of his surroundings again, he saw Jenna looking at him in concern. Smiling, he shrugged the vision off for now. He would worry about the vision later. Right now, his family was his top priority.

He stiffened when he felt Phoenix touch his mind. *I don't know what the fuck just happened, but you will tell me later, my brother.*

Nico gave a slight nod and stopped the swing. Grabbing Lily and throwing her up into the air, he caught her, and then swung her around in a circle. He was deliberately distracting her because he didn't want her to somehow catch his thoughts. When Jenna called out that it was time to eat, he took Lily over to her and grinned, "It looks great! I'm starving."

As everyone gathered around and sat down to eat, Hunter suddenly changed. One minute, he was a little bear cub, and the next he was a five-year-old boy with curly brown hair and dark brown eyes, who desperately needed a pair of pants. With a laugh, Jenna handed him some jogging pants and a tee shirt, and Phoenix helped him slip them on.

Hunter didn't say a word. He just snuggled up on Phoenix's lap and waited for Jenna to give him his lunch. His eyes grew round at the amount of food she put on his plate, but he ate every last bit of it. Then, he tugged Phoenix over to the swing so he could have his turn.

25

Later on that evening, all of Angel's team had gone home except for Phoenix. He'd brought a bag with him the night before, and planned on staying with Nico as long as his friend needed him. Or until Jenna kicked him out, whichever came first.

What most people didn't know was that Nico and Phoenix had been friends for years. They were in the military together and, at one time, Nico had saved Phoenix's life. He'd taken a bullet for Phoenix that would have killed him, but with Nico's shifter abilities, even though it had hurt like a bitch, it had not mortally wounded him. That was how Phoenix found out about shifters. Afterwards, he hid Nico and kept him safe for several days until he was physically capable of fighting again, and then they returned to camp with a story about getting separated from their team and being lost. They had been inseparable since then. RARE was the family Phoenix had never had. Nico was the brother he'd always wanted. And there wasn't anything he would not do for him.

Phoenix sat on the back porch drinking one of the beers that Jenna had stocked the fridge with while they were gone. He was waiting for Nico. He didn't know what the hell had happened earlier in the day while they were on the picnic, but he was damn well going to find out. He had seen the vacant look come into Nico's eyes first. The one he always got when a vision started. Then had come the terror and stark fear. He didn't know what was up with that, but he was not going to bed until he found out. He had plenty of patience, and he would sit out on the porch steps and wait until Nico was ready to talk about it.

While he waited, he watched Storm cross the lawn to him. She sat down beside him, crossing her arms over her legs as she pulled them up to her chest. Silently, he handed her the extra beer he had brought out for Nico. What the hell, Nico wouldn't be out anytime soon. She nodded her thanks, and tilting back her head, took a long drink. As he watched her throat move as she swallowed, his dick jumped to attention in his jeans. Oh shit. Shifters could smell lust couldn't they?

"Stay close to Nico," Storm said softly, still not looking at Phoenix. "There's going to come a time when he is going to need you. Be there for him when he does, and I will come for you," she promised.

I would like to come for you right now, Phoenix thought, fighting the urge to readjust his dick.

"I would give my life for him," Phoenix said out loud.

"It won't come to that," she promised. "Just remember, no matter what, I will come for you." Storm turned and looked him directly in the eyes. And then, cupping his face in her hands, she pulled him to her and kissed him softly on the lips. Tears filling her eyes, she stood. "I'm so sorry it has to be this way," she whispered, "but he will die if you don't do this." Reaching out, she trailed a hand across his shaved head and down the side of his face. Then she leaned down and kissed him softly on the head, gently nuzzled his cheek, and turned and walked away.

What the fuck was that about, Phoenix thought as he tried to will his hard-on away. Be there for Nico. Hells to the yeah, he would be there for his brother, no matter what. But when had hard ass Storm the Enforcer become Storm the beautiful, sexy woman he wanted to fuck? He reached down and palmed his erection trying to move it into a less painful position, and groaned loudly when he about shot in his pants. What the fuck?

26

Nico silently slipped out of bed and pulled on a pair of shorts from one of the bags Phoenix had packed him, knowing there was no way Nico was leaving his family again.

"Where are you going?" his mate whispered softly.

"Just going to talk to Phoenix for a bit," he said.

"Check on the kids, will you?" she asked.

Hunter was staying the night with them, too. He was sleeping on a small twin bed that had been moved into the spare bedroom Phoenix was using. They were going to have to talk to the council about what to do with him eventually, but for now, he would stay with them and Phoenix. "I will, sweet mate," he promised, leaning over to kiss her softly.

He went to Lily's room first. She was sound asleep in bed, snuggling with Shadow and her blanket, snoring softly. Crossing the room, he placed a soft kiss on the top of her head, pulling her comforter up to her shoulders.

Next, he checked on Hunter. Hunter must have shifted

in his sleep. He had gone to bed as a little boy, but now his clothes were shredded and he was curled up in a ball at the end of the bed, once again in his bear cub form. Nico silently shut the door so that he wouldn't disturb him and moved on.

He found Phoenix out on the back porch lost in thought. The beer bottle sitting beside him was empty. Another set on the other side of the steps, just over halfway full. Nico sat down beside him, raising an eyebrow. "Did you have company tonight?"

"Yeah," Phoenix said roughly, leaving it at that.

Nico inhaled and then grinned. "Storm come to see ya, did she?" Phoenix looked over at him, and the smile left Nico's face. "Hey man, what's wrong?"

Phoenix glanced away, rubbed his head, and then looked back. "What happened today, brother? At the picnic? Talk to me."

Now it was Nico's turn to look away. "Shit, Phoenix, you don't want to know." Phoenix just waited, watching him. "I had a vision. A really fucked-up vision. We were in the jungle fighting some of the General's army. That's what they were, too, a fucking army. We were fighting them, and then I took a bullet in the chest. The bastards got me, threw me into a helicopter, and took off. None of you could get to me in time. You were too far away. I heard them say that the General would be happy. That I would make a good addition to his program. His fucking breeding program. First of all, I have a mate. I can't have sex with anyone else but my mate. It just won't happen. I doubt it physically could, but I would never do that to Jenna. They would have to kill me first."

As Phoenix watched Nico look out across the lawn, he

understood what Storm had meant now. He had to be there to take that bullet. It would kill Nico if he took it, not because the bullet would kill him, but because if he got put into that program and would not or could not perform, eventually the General would have him killed. He took a deep breath. He could do this. For his brother, for his brother's family, he would do this.

"Tell me everything you remember about the vision," he told Nico. "Describe where we were, where you were standing when you took the bullet, everything. This is one vision we are going to prevent from happening." As Nico talked, Phoenix mentally stored the information in his mind to take out and go over later. He would go over it all again and again, until he was sure he knew exactly what had happened, and exactly where he needed to be at the right time to make sure that he was the one that took that bullet and was taken by the General's men instead of Nico. He didn't give a shit about what happened to him after that. All he cared about was keeping Nico safe and with his family.

27

The next day, Jenna decided it was time for her to go back to work. She worked for Chase as his personal assistant, but with everything that had happened with Lily, she had not been in for days. Chase had been staying late into the night, trying to keep up with everything. And even though he never complained, she could tell that he was exhausted. She was going to take Lily with her, but Nico said he would keep her until he had his meeting with Angel and the team that afternoon.

As Jenna was getting ready to leave, there was a knock on the door. When she opened it, Angel and the rest of the team were standing there beside a brand new bright pink Barbie bike with training wheels. "We weren't sure if Lily knew how to ride a bike, or even if she had one, but we wanted to get her a welcome to the family present," Angel said.

Jenna's eyes filled with tears as she looked at the bike. "No, she doesn't have one," she whispered. "Thank you so

much, she's going to love it." She felt an arm go around
her waist and turned to Nico with a warm smile. He
leaned down and kissed her softly.

Phoenix moved into the doorway with the bear cub on
his hip and Lily's hand in his. Lily squealed as she saw the
bike. "It's mine?" she asked jumping up and down, her
pigtails bobbing all over the place. Pig tails? Who had
done Lily's hair in pig tails?

As the team laughed, Angel told the excited girl, "Yes,
it's yours. And we thought if it was okay with your
mommy, we would all hang out here with you this
morning while she went to work, and we could teach you
how to ride it."

Jenna's eyes widened in surprise, but then she caught
on quickly. They weren't just here to give Lily the bike.
They were here to support Nico and Jenna, and to protect
Lily. The whole team had shown up, all of them, to
protect her child. For the longest time it had been just
Chase, Jenna, and Lily. Granted, they had the pack, but
when it came to personal things, they only relied on each
other. After what happened with Walker, Jenna had closed
herself off from all of her friends. She spent time with
Chase and Lily, but that was pretty much it. She didn't
even talk to Toni anymore. She had been so lonely before
Nico came into her life. Now she not only had Chase,
Lily, and Nico, but she had Angel and her team, too. Their
little family had more than just doubled. "Please, stay as
long as you can," Jenna said, a tremulous smile crossing
her face. "We can grill out for dinner. I have some steak in
the freezer."

"That would be great," Angel grinned, and the others

agreed. "We also have something for you, Jenna." Reaching into her pocket, she took out a bright red cell phone. Handing it to Jenna she told her, "This phone has all of our phone numbers programmed into it. If you need anything, anything at all, day or night, you call one of us. We will be there. Welcome to the family, Jenna." Jenna stared at the phone for a long moment, and then looked back up at Angel. She slowly reached out and took the phone from the other woman, and put it in her purse.

"Chase, too?" She asked quietly.

"Chase?" Angel asked, her brow furrowing in confusion.

"Is Chase welcome, too?" Jenna asked.

Angel smiled warmly at her. "Chase is a part of your family, Jenna. That makes him a part of ours. Of course, Chase, too."

Unable to stop herself, Jenna threw her arms around Angel and whispered, "Thank you. You don't know how much all of this means to me."

Angel hugged her back for a moment and then told her, "You better get to work before you get fired. I hear your boss is a real tyrant."

Chuckling, Jenna pulled back. She turned and gave Nico a kiss and then walked away toward the building she and Chase worked out of. Looking back at Angel and her team, she smiled and waved, and then turned back around and hurried to work.

As he watched Jenna go, Nico thanked Angel. He was thanking her not only for the gifts she had brought Jenna and Lily, but for openly accepting them all into their family. They had never allowed anyone on the 'outside' in their little group before. It meant more people to care about, more people to protect, more people to give their lives for if the time came. And they would do it, because to them, that was what family did.

28

The team spent all morning playing. It had been way too long since they took the time to do anything that was fun. They helped Lily and Hunter take turns riding Lily's new bike. They played in the back yard on the swing set. It was a larger swing set, so Angel and Rikki were able to swing and go down the slide with the kids. And after that, they all played kickball. They even debated on taking the kids over to the park, but decided it might bring back too many memories for Lily. She seemed to be doing better, and they didn't want to trigger anything.

At noon they ate lunch, and then Angel decided it was time that she went and checked in at the hospital. She wanted to see how Flame, Janie, and the two wolf pups were doing. And, yes, she could admit it to herself only, she wanted to see Chase. The mate pull was strong and hard to ignore. She was hoping that maybe a few minutes spent with him would calm her wolf. Her wolf, on the other hand, wanted to find him and jump his bones, the horny bitch.

As Angel neared the hospital, she noticed that Janie was sitting outside on a bench by some flowers. She was rubbing her belly and singing softly. Angel glanced around and saw two enforcers standing by the hospital building, casually leaning up against it. Good, Chase had guards watching over Janie.

When Angel went over and sat down beside her, Janie stopped singing, but her hand never left her belly. They sat in silence for a while, and then Janie slowly reached out her other hand and grabbed hold of one of Angel's.

Covering the other woman's hand with one of hers, Angel asked quietly, "Is there anyone I can call for you, Janie?" Janie seemed to hesitate, before shaking her head. "You must have family somewhere looking for you," Angel tried again softly. Once again, Janie shook her head.

"There is no one," she said quietly, looking up at Angel, her eyes full of sadness. "I'm a latent wolf shifter. I was kicked out of my pack because I can't shift. I made it for a full year on my own before the General and his men found me. They had me for two years before you rescued me. I don't even know why they took me. I can't shift, and I have no idea if my baby will be able to, but he would not let me go."

Janie was trembling, and Angel could smell the fear radiating off of her, but she was talking. That was a huge step. As far as Angel knew, Janie hadn't said a word since they arrived at the compound. Angel wanted to kill the bastards that had hurt this gentle, frightened woman.

"Do you think they will make me leave, Angel?" she asked with tears in her eyes. "I don't have anywhere to go. I don't have anywhere safe to take my baby."

"You have a place in my pack now if you want one," a

deep voice said. "You and your pup will always be safe and protected here."

Janie's head snapped around, and she watched Chase through lowered eyes. "Alpha," she whispered, the terror evident in her voice.

"You will never be hurt here, Janie. Never be made to do anything you do not want to do. There is no need to be afraid. You are safe now." The truth was in his voice, in his vow to her. He would not let anyone hurt her ever again. She was one of his now, and he protected what was his. Chase let loose some of his power. He let it roll over Janie and comfort her.

Janie looked at Angel with both hope and fear in her eyes. When Angel nodded reassuringly, smiling warmly, Janie turned back to Chase with a small smile and grateful eyes. "Thank you, Alpha. I accept your offer. I would like to join your pack."

Chase just nodded, a soft, gentle smile on his lips. "Your apartment is ready for you, Janie. We are giving you a two bedroom so that you will have a nursery for the baby."

She looked at him in shock. "You mean I get my own place?" she asked incredulously.

"Of course," he responded. "Unless you don't want to be alone? If not, then there are several single female wolves that can stay with you. We can put the baby in your room, or we can upgrade to a three bedroom so you would both have your own room and the baby would have a nursery. I think there is one still available. I would need to ask Jenna."

"No, no," Janie said quickly. "A two bedroom is fine.

But, maybe Flame could stay with me? If she wants to, that is. I would feel safe with her."

"We can ask her," Chase agreed. Angel's heart jumped in her chest when he finally looked in her direction. "Would you like to come with me to talk to Flame?" he asked her.

Angel nodded, rising to her feet and letting go of Janie's hand. "We are going to grill out tonight at Nico and Jenna's if you would like to come over, Janie," Angel told her.

Janie nodded slowly, "Okay, if you are sure you want me there."

Angel leaned over and gave her a quick hug, running a hand gently down her hair. "I will see you there."

"Sable and Charlotte will come with you, Janie," Chase said gesturing over to where the enforcers stood. "They are your guards for now until we know for sure that you are safe."

Janie looked at him in surprise, her gaze going quickly back to the enforcers. Her fear was a bitter, acrid smell. Sable and Charlotte stayed where they were, but Charlotte said softly, "Ma'am, we are here to watch out for you, nothing more. We will not come near you unless you need us."

Janie's fear subsided somewhat, and she whispered, "Okay."

Chase and Angel told Janie goodbye, and then turned and went up the stairs and into the hospital. As they made their way toward Flame's room, they heard her yell, "I don't care what you want, I refuse to stay in this bed any longer. Now get the hell out of my way!"

Angel chuckled softly, "There's my Flame!" When Chase raised his eyebrows at her, she told him, "She's as feisty as they come. Doesn't take shit from anyone. I was afraid those bastards would break her before I could get her out of there. The things that woman went through, Chase. Bran is going to need to have a lot of patience. Hell, I don't know if she will ever be ready for a relationship. I know I'm not."

As Chase's head snapped around to her, she realized what she had just let slip. He growled low in his throat, "Who hurt you?" Angel shook her head and continued down the hall. Chase reached out and grabbed her wrist, pulling her into an empty room and pushing her back up against the door so no one could come in. "Who...hurt... you?" He ground out slowly.

"Back the fuck off, Chase," Angel growled, twisting out of his grip and moving to stand behind a chair by the window. He didn't move, just stood there watching her, hands clenched like he wanted to hit something. She turned back to him and sighed, "It doesn't matter. It is what it is. It was a long time ago. And I killed the asshole. I made sure he could never come after me again. But you need to realize something, Chase. A part of me wants you, my wolf definitely wants you, but there is another part of me that may never be able to commit to you. That part of me never wants a mate. She never wants to let anyone that close, close enough to hurt her, again."

"You let your team in. You consider them your family now," Chase said.

"It's not the same thing," Angel argued. "I trust them with my life. They aren't a threat to me."

"And you will never trust me," Chase muttered, his eyes dark with anger. "You consider me a threat. I am your mate, Angel. I would care for you, I would honor and cherish you, I would do anything for you, and I would never hurt you."

Angel closed her eyes tightly, her hands gripping the back of the chair she stood behind. She took a deep breath, and when she opened her eyes, Chase was gone. Well, that went great.

29

A ngel sat in the chair in the empty hospital room and waited a good twenty minutes before she finally got up and headed once again toward Flame's room. She paused outside the door, watching Flame gaze out the window. She was alone, which surprised Angel. She had thought Chase would either still be with her, or at least Bran would be.

"I made everyone leave," Flame said, turning toward her. "Stupid fucking idiots. Trying to tell me what I can and cannot do. Not gonna happen. Those bastards that held me for months did it, and no one will ever do that to me again."

"If it wasn't for them, you might not be here now," Angel said, wincing at the acrid scent of fear and pain in the room. "They are just trying to help you. Should you even be out of bed yet, Flame?" When Flame didn't reply, Angel raised an eyebrow. "Look, I understand how you feel, and I'm not trying to push you or anything, but it has only been a day. You aren't a shifter, and you don't heal like we do. I can tell you are in a lot of pain right now."

Flame sighed deeply, slipping into the chair by the window. "No, probably not. It does hurt. Badly. But, I can't just sit here. God, Angel. It was horrible. So horrible." A shudder worked its way through her body, and she seemed to close in on herself.

"Do you want to talk about it?" Angel asked quietly.

Flame looked up at her and shook her head. "I can't. I'm sorry, I just can't. Not yet. All I can tell you is that I finally accepted the baby inside of me, grew to love him after the first couple of months of hating him, and now he's gone. And I swear to you, Angel, that I am going to kill every last son of a bitch that had a part in hurting me and my son. I am going to tear them apart."

"Revenge is a cold and lonely road, my friend," Angel said.

"Not from where I stand," Flame responded. "It's fiery hot, filled with flames. And they are all going to burn. Teach me, Angel, please. Teach me what I need to know to protect myself."

"To protect yourself or to get your revenge?"

"They go hand in hand," Flame replied.

Angel eyed her for a moment, before nodding in agreement. It was obvious that if Angel didn't train her, Flame would either find someone that would, or she would rush out halfcocked and get herself killed. "Fine, you stay in this bed until the doctor says it's all right for you to leave, and once she gives her approval, the team and I will train you. But, it isn't going to be all cupcakes and pony rides, Sister. It is going to be hard work. And one more thing…you have to tell Bran."

"Tell Bran? Why would I have to tell him?" Flame argued.

"Because he's your mate, Flame, and no matter what, mates come first," Angel said.

"Like you put your mate first?" Flame sneered.

Angel rose to her full height, looking down at Flame in the chair. "Disrespect me like that again and you will need to find someone else to train you," she growled. "And stay the fuck out of my head." Angel turned and walked out of Flame's room, ignoring the other woman's protests.

What sucked was that Flame was right. Chase was her mate. He should be first in every aspect of her life, but she was scared to death to allow him anywhere near her heart. And that just pissed her off. Angel did not do fear anymore. She hadn't allowed it to be a part of her life for years.

Angel made her way to the other end of the hall where the wolf pups were. They had changed back last night into beautiful twin little girls with long blond hair and big blue eyes. As Angel opened the door, her eyes narrowed when she heard them whimpering.

"Angel," Doc Josie called out. Angel stopped with the door half opened and turned to look at her. "They haven't let anyone get near them since last night. It was a fight to get them bathed and in pajamas, and today they are hiding in the closet. They won't come out. We decided the best course of action is to just back off and leave them alone for a while."

Angel nodded to the doctor, and then pushed the door the rest of the way open and walked into the room.

"You don't listen to anything you don't want to, do you?" the doctor growled.

"Nope," Angel said. "Now get out." She pushed the door shut on the doctor's pissed off expression. She didn't need Doc Josie in the room ruining any chance she had of calming the pups down.

Angel walked across the room and sat down in the rocking chair facing the window. As she gazed out at the beautiful garden of flowers in the back of the hospital, she tried to think of a way to get the children to come out and talk to her. She had seen the jammies thrown on the floor, so she knew they had changed back to pups. That meant they were frightened. She knew they felt safer in their wolf forms. As she rocked, she started to hum softly and then began to sing a soft lullaby. When she moved on from 'Twinkle Twinkle Little Star' to 'Incy Wincy Spider', she heard movement behind her. Not turning around to look at them, she finished that song and started 'Jesus Loves Me'. All of a sudden, her lap was full of two little wolf pups. Angel gathered them close, and closing her eyes, she kept on singing. They sat in silence after the last song, Angel gently stroking their fur. Her arms had been empty for so long. When they fell asleep, she sat and rocked them, holding them for hours, remembering another little girl she used to rock all night long.

A nurse peeked in on them in the afternoon, but quickly moved back out when she saw the pups asleep in Angel's arms. Around 5:30 p.m., they started to stir. Softly Angel said, "How about you two change back to little girls and we break out of this place? I know another girl and a boy that would love to play with you." One minute she was snuggling two wolf pups, the next she had two little blond girls in her arms.

Slowly, Angel stood up and walked over to sit them on

the bed. They watched her cross over and pick their jammies up off the floor, their eyes never leaving her. Angel quickly dressed them, wrapping them both in blankets, and then picked them up. The brisk April air was still chilly outside, and she did not want them to get cold on the way to Jenna's.

As she walked out of the room with them, Doc Josie smiled at her. "I didn't think you would be able to do it," she admitted.

"I know," Angel told her. "I'm breaking them out of here. We have a party to head off to."

Grinning, the doctor asked, "Will they be back tonight?"

Angel held them close, whispering, "I don't know, Doc. I don't know."

30

Nico and the team waited for Angel to come back to the cottage for their meeting, but she never showed. When they tried to call her, it went straight to voice mail. Nico was worried, but he also knew that if Angel needed them, she would reach out telepathically.

Chase and Jenna arrived that evening, and they brought Janie with them. She sat back away from everyone, but watched them all closely. Every once in a while, she would smile at something the children did or said, but she stayed quiet

As the sun began to set, Phoenix started the grill in the backyard and the team watched the children play while they talked. They still had not heard from Angel. Deciding he was tired of waiting to see if she was going to call, Nico asked Chase if he had any idea where she was. Chase frowned in confusion. "No, I haven't seen her since the hospital right after lunch."

"She never came back," Nico told him. "We were supposed to have a meeting this afternoon, but she never showed up, and she isn't answering her phone. That's not like her."

"I'll call the hospital to see if she is still there, or if she mentioned where she was going when she left."

Just as Chase picked up his phone, Jenna said, "Here she comes."

All eyes turned to watch Angel make her way toward them holding two little bundles. She walked over to where Chase sat on a glider swing and slowly lowered herself down beside him. The little girls had their heads buried in her neck and refused to look at anyone.

"Hey now," Angel said softly. "This is my family. You are safe here. I promise." After a moment, they slowly raised their heads and glanced around. They were trembling, but they bravely took everything in as they clung to Angel. She gently kissed them both on the cheek and then turned them to look at Chase. "This is Chase. He's the alpha here, and he will protect you."

Their eyes widened as they stared at him nervously. "He won't hurt us?" one of them whispered.

"Never," Angel promised. "He will never hurt you, nor will he allow anyone else to."

Chase slowly reached out and ran a knuckle gently down first one little girl's cheek, and then the other. "No one will ever hurt you again," he promised them. They watched him for a minute and then one of them climbed over onto his lap and laid her head on his shoulder, the other staying with Angel.

Nico watched them and felt fury roll through him. These little girls were scared to death of everyone. Janie was terrified to be around anyone. Flame was still in the hospital because of what had happened to her. And his

Jenna, his beautiful mate, had gone through so much at the hands of the General. What the hell kind of monster was he?

The kind that deserves to be sent straight to hell, and will be just as soon as we find him, Angel whispered into his mind.

Nico looked over at her, gritting his teeth and nodded slightly. He knew his eyes had gone wolf, and he was fighting to control it, but it was so hard. In an effort to distract himself, he asked Angel, "What are their names?" Angel glanced down at them, frowning as she shrugged her shoulders slightly.

"We don't have names," one of the little girls murmured. "Our mommy died when we were born, and we didn't get any names."

Phoenix walked over and knelt down in front of them. "Of course, you have names," he said with a gentle smile. "You are Faith and Hope."

One of the children's eyes widened as she looked at him. "We are?"

"Yep, little Faith, you are," he replied. She smiled; a smile that lit up her whole face.

Her sister whispered in awe, "My name is Hope." Phoenix nodded at her and grinned.

Chase snuggled Hope closer to him and said, "And what beautiful names they are."

Angel looked over at Chase, wishing she could tell him what a wonderful man she thought he was, and how she wished she could be what he wanted, but he didn't even look at her. That hurt. Yes, she was the one who had said she did not think she could be his mate, not now, not ever. But his rejection hurt so much. She wanted to lean into him, and for once let someone else shoulder her pain and responsibilities. She wanted someone to share her burdens with. Someone to hold her and tell her everything was going to be all right, and that she wasn't alone. She wanted her mate.

Angel sat in silence, watching everyone else as they talked and joked. And she watched the other kids as they played on the swing set. She was so tired, just so exhausted. She hadn't snagged more than a couple of hours of sleep here and there in days. Giving into temptation, she did the only thing she really wanted to do. Leaning into her mate, she closed her eyes, sagging against him, praying that he didn't fully reject her in front of everyone. *It's not that I don't trust you, Chase*, she whispered into his mind. *It's just that I am scared to death that I can't be what you want. What you need. I have too many issues, too many ghosts.*

Chase held himself stiffly for a moment before moving Hope over to his other shoulder and slipping his arm around Angel, pulling her closer. "Why don't you let me be the judge of that?" he whispered. Sitting there holding precious little Faith while Chase held her, Angel could not resist anymore, and she slowly drifted off to sleep in her mate's arms. She dreamt of another precious little girl that she had held like this so many years ago, unaware of the tears that escaped, sliding down her cheeks.

———

ANGEL WOKE up still snuggled in Chase's arms, but the girls had been coaxed out to play with the other children. They were running around in their jammies, but had jackets on that had obviously come from Lily. It warmed

Angel's heart to hear their giggles. "We need to find a place for them to stay," she said quietly. "I don't want them to have to live at the hospital."

Janie spoke up, "They can stay with me, if you want?"

Everything in Angel rebelled at the idea and she stiffened in Chase's arms. *No, they are my babies.* She knew she was being stupid, but she wanted the girls with her. She had claimed them in that hospital chair where she sat for hours holding them. It had been so long since she'd opened her heart to anyone, but those little girls had stolen it within the first five minutes they were in her lap.

"Thanks, Janie," Chase said, running a hand gently down Angel's arm. "I appreciate the offer, but I think I will have them stay with me for now." He had heard her, and he was going to keep the girls for her. Angel was in so much pain. It was pain that she hid from everyone, but he knew. He did not know what had happened to her, but he was hoping that he would get the chance to find out. He knew she was the badass leader of RARE, but he also knew there was a softer, deeper side to her, too. And he wanted all of her.

Jenna looked over in surprise. "Are you sure, Chase? They could stay with us."

"They will stay with me," he repeated firmly. "They will be fine. I will get a live-in nanny…" Before he could finish that thought, Angel's claws were out, digging into his leg, and her growl was deadly. "Or not," he said chuckling. He wasn't sure if she was upset because she did not want the pups around another woman, or if it was because she didn't want him around one, but he knew which one he was hoping for. "While I'm at work, they can go to the daycare, unless Angel is around and wouldn't mind keeping them company."

Angel's nails retracted slowly, and the growling stopped. Damn, he was hoping it was him she was jealous over, not the pups.

It was both, Asshat, he heard. Chase's laughter shook his whole frame, as he leaned over and nuzzled her cheek, and then kissed her softly on the forehead. He immediately realized his mistake when he felt her begin to retreat from him.

"Let's eat," Phoenix yelled, interrupting the moment.

As everyone grabbed plates and filled them with food, Angel got up and moved away from Chase, erecting the shield around her heart once more. When she felt like she was once again in charge of her emotions, she said, "RARE has a meeting at 9 p.m. tonight. I need Ryker and Storm there, Chase. Please find someone to take their places on Jenna and Lily's security detail until we get back." She saw Phoenix stiffen at that. Interesting. As she watched him out of the corner of her eye, she caught him looking at Nico with a determined look on his face. Even more interesting. Nico glanced over at Phoenix and shook his head once. Okay, she was all over that shit now. She had always tried hard to stay out of her team's heads, but if they didn't spill their little secret tonight, all bets were off. When it came to the safety of her family, she would do whatever it took.

Angel wasn't the only one that was watching Phoenix and Nico's exchange. More than one person on the team wanted to find out what was up with the two of them... and they would, in their own ways.

Once everything was cleaned up from dinner, the

team piled into the SUV and headed out to Angel's house, Storm and Ryker following on their motorcycles. It was a good forty minutes away, but they needed a private place where they could come up with their next plan of action without the distraction of cubs, pups, and mates. And if Angel was honest with herself, it was away from Chase and the confusion he made her feel.

She knew he had kept Hope and Faith for her, and Angel wanted it all. She wanted her mate, she wanted the girls, and she wanted the white house with the picket fence. But she just did not know how to make that happen. Even if she could somehow get over her messed up past, how would she ever keep them all safe in her line of work. She made enemies. Granted, most of the time they ghosted in and out and no one had a clue who they were. But, they had made a name for themselves. And there was every chance that someone could come hunting for them at any time. How could she protect Chase and the girls if someone found out about them? Shaking her head, Angel pushed the thoughts from her mind. It was too dangerous to contemplate a life with her mate. She had to keep her distance, so he and the girls were safe.

31

Everyone sat around the huge table in Angel's basement. The room looked just like a conference room you would find in an executive building. It even had a large dry erase board across one wall. This was their planning room. It was where they met, tossed around ideas, and came up with their plans to kick ass and take names. It was not the most comfortable room, but they weren't there to kick back and watch movies. Comfort did not really matter.

Nico watched as Storm and Ryker glanced around the room, taking it all in. The enforcers had worked with RARE in the past, but they had never been a part of the team before. They had always been on the sidelines, helping out as needed. Nico had a feeling that was about to change.

Jaxson set up his computer, and Angel gave everyone else a pen and a pad of paper. "All right, first things first." Angel looked directly at Nico. "Are you and your buddy going to tell us all what is going on, or do I need to find out for myself?"

Well fuck. That was just like Angel. Don't hold anything back. "Not much to tell," Nico responded evasively.

"You really don't want to go there with me right now, Nico. Everyone in this room is aware that something is going on. I want to know what it is, and I want to know now. We don't keep secrets on this team. We can't survive that way."

Crap, Angel was pissed. He had really been hoping that none of this would come up. He could handle it. He didn't have a solution yet, but he would.

"Just a vision Nico had, Angel," Phoenix said with a shrug.

"And?" Angel persisted.

Phoenix glanced quickly at Nico and then back to her, but stayed silent.

"Nico is going to get taken," Storm interjected. All eyes turned toward her. And just like that, Phoenix was done with her. Nico and Phoenix had each other's backs no matter what. And any woman that he ended up with would understand that. Storm was giving away information they had wanted to keep to themselves. Phoenix would have taken Nico's spot and everything would have been fine, which was exactly what Storm had told him to do. But now that the entire team was aware of what was going on, shit was going to hit the fan. Yep, his dick wasn't getting hard for her again.

"It's nothing," Nico growled. "Phoenix and I are going to handle it."

"No, you aren't," Angel snapped, her eyes darkening in anger. "We are all going to handle it. Now talk."

Nico and Phoenix stared at each other for a moment, and then Nico did the only thing that he could do. He talked. He told them of his vision, told them everything he had told Phoenix, except for one thing. When they wanted to know exactly where he was when all of this happened in his vision, he answered them very vaguely. They would have known if he was lying, but technically he wasn't. He just didn't give them the detailed description he had given Phoenix. When he was finished, Angel grimaced and said, "Okay, this is one vision that definitely is not going to come true. You will not be taken, Nico. I refuse to let your mate and child lose you. I refuse to lose you."

Nico swallowed hard and nodded once, taking a long drink of his soda. "That's good, Angel, because I don't want to be lost."

Angel squeezed his shoulder, muttering, "You won't be," before turning to look at Jaxson. "Okay, Jax, you're up. Talk to us."

"I sifted through everything that I got off of the computer in Tijuana. It took a while because it was encrypted, but it looks like he has women stashed in different areas all around the globe. The sick fuck is trying to breed them. I'm not sure what he is hoping to accomplish. It looked like at first, he was just breeding psychics to psychics, but then he found out about shifters. Now he is focused on breeding shifters with psychics. I honestly don't know what his end game is. It seems like he is breeding his own army. But, I'm not sure why. I can't find any proof that the government is actually involved. It looks as if it is all him. But that doesn't make sense. Where is he getting his backing from?"

"That's something we need to look further into. How many different places have you found where he has women?" Angel asked.

"Looks like eighteen places so far," Jaxson responded. "There could be more. Wait, make that seventeen. Phoenix blew one of them up already."

"Looks like I got seventeen more to go," Phoenix said. "Point the fuckers out."

As the rest of the team loudly agreed, Angel held up a hand. "How many women are out there, Jax? How many women are in these places like Flame and Janie?"

"Most of them are smaller and only have two to three women in them. But there is one that is a lot bigger, and it looks like it has twenty-three women in it right now. I think that is where he is holding them until they get pregnant, and then he is shipping them off to the other places to be monitored by scientists until the children are born," Jaxson responded.

"Fuck me," Trace growled. "We are hitting that place first. You put me and Rikki in place, Angel. We will go hunting."

"I'm right there with ya," Rikki said. "That sick bastard. I can't believe he is doing that to all of those women!"

"Look," Angel interrupted, holding up a hand, "I understand how you feel, I really do. But I think it would be smarter if we went in and picked off the smaller places one-by-one first. Take out the tentacles of the monster, and then go after him."

"What about all of those women that are being raped right now?" Rikki insisted. "We have a chance to get them out of there before they become pregnant. We need to move before they are sent to one of those places where we found Flame and Janie. They could be violated again while they are pregnant, this time suffering even more."

"And what about the women that are already pregnant and in the smaller facilities? The ones who are currently being hurt, possibly raped, and are scared to death that they are going to lose their babies?" Storm argued.

"If we hit the smaller facilities first, they will know we found out where they all are and could possibly move the main facility," Nico pointed out. "Of course, if we hit the bigger facility then they could move all of the smaller ones, too."

"It would be harder to relocate all of the smaller ones," Jaxson pointed out. "If we hit the bigger one first, it will take longer for them to move the smaller ones."

Angel sighed, "This is bigger than us, guys. Bigger than anything we have taken on before. We are going to have to ask for help on this one. Storm and Ryker, we will get you the locations of the smaller facilities. Get a hold of the council and see if they will send enforcers to all of them. RARE will hit the biggest one. I want to move on this as early as the day after tomorrow, so find out if they can be ready by then. We need to hit them all at the same time for it to work."

Ryker got on his phone and contacted the council immediately, while Storm told Jaxson where to send the information. When Ryker finished the call, he told them, "The council is in. Send the information to us. We will be ready to hit the places within two days. Storm and I need to leave now so that we can get everything set up on our end, but we will be in touch."

As they walked out, Storm glanced back at Phoenix, but he would not even acknowledge her. That ship had sailed. He wasn't wasting his time on the wrong ones anymore. He wanted to find the right one, and he now knew for sure that it was not her.

"All right everyone, it's late. Let's get out of here. Meet back at 10 o'clock tomorrow morning so we can come up with a plan. Phoenix and Nico, take my SUV. I won't need it tonight."

When Angel began to pick up the pop cans and snacks everyone had, Rikki waved her away. "I got this, girl." She grabbed a trash can and started throwing everything into it, so Angel followed the others up the stairs to kick them all out.

When Rikki came up, she took the trash out with her toward the dumpster, and Angel shut and locked the door. Going into her bedroom, she collapsed on her bed, not even bothering to remove her clothes. She was exhausted. She fell asleep, dreaming of Chase, Hope, and Faith, and of the family she wished they could be.

32

Jenna sighed when she felt Nico crawl into bed behind her. She slid back, snuggling up closer to him, and moaned softly when she felt his hand trail down her naked breast, stopping to lightly tweak her nipple. She felt his hard cock pressing against her and growled softly, wanting to feel it inside of her. She tried to position herself so that he could slide easily in, but he grabbed her by the hips and held her so she couldn't move. "Nico, please," she breathed.

Nico laughed softly, kissing her behind her ear and trailing more kisses down her neck to her shoulder. "Slow down, love."

Jenna groaned, shoving back against him. "Nico, I need you. Please, I need to feel you inside me."

Nico growled softly, biting down gently on Jenna's shoulder, holding her in place. Then he pulled one of her legs up and pushed slowly inside of her. Continuing to move slowly, he slid in and out of her. She jerked her hips back to try and get him to move faster, but he refused. "I'm making love to you this time, my sweet mate. I want to show you how much you mean to me," he whispered.

"Nico," she cried out as she felt the pressure building inside of her. He reached down and massaged her clit, and she slid her arm up and behind her, grabbing hold of his head, pulling his lips back to her shoulder. "God, Nico," she begged, "bite me. Please, bite me."

Nico could not resist. As his fangs entered her shoulder, he felt her squeeze tightly around him, and he couldn't hold back. Grabbing her hips, he slammed into her once, then twice, and then came hard.

"I love you, my sweet mate," he whispered. "I love you so much."

Jenna froze and then she leaned back and looked up into his eyes. "I love you, too, Nico," she whispered.

Turning her around to face him, Nico held her close and kissed her softly. As she drifted off to sleep, she felt him gently stroking her hair and heard him whisper, "Never forget how much I love you."

The next morning Nico woke her up and made love to her again. This time Jenna felt what seemed like desperation in him. It was fast and hard, and so different than the night before. But when she asked him about it afterwards, he shrugged it off. "Come on, Sweetheart, Phoenix is cooking again," he teased. "Do you think he made you a bunny?"

Jenna laughed, but she felt the underlying tension in him. She had no idea what was wrong with her mate, and it was driving her crazy.

As they walked out of the bedroom, Nico stopped and

turned toward her. Placing a hand on her cheek, he whispered, "I do love you, Jenna."

Her eyes filled with tears as she looked up at him. "Talk to me, Nico," she whispered, fear filling her at the tone of his voice. "What's wrong?"

He leaned his forehead onto hers and sighed softly. "We are leaving on a mission very soon. You never know what could happen. I just want to make sure you know how I feel."

Jenna stared at him in silence, watching him closely. "You do know, Nico," she suddenly realized. "You know. Tell me! What's going to happen? Talk to me, dammit!"

"Nothing is going to happen," Phoenix vowed from behind Nico. "Nothing. We are going on a mission and Nico will be home in a couple of days."

"Promise me, Phoenix," Jenna demanded.

Phoenix looked her straight in the eyes and vowed, "I promise you. I give you my word, Jenna. Your mate will be home as soon as the mission is over."

Jenna glanced back and forth between Phoenix and Nico, before finally nodding. "Good. Now, where's my bunny?"

Phoenix threw his head back and laughed, "Lily is saving it for you, along with a pile of bacon. Go eat."

Once she was in the kitchen, Nico turned to Phoenix and punched him in the arm. "What the fuck man?" he growled. "How can you promise her that? I told you about my vision, and you know they always come true."

"Not this time, Nico. No fucking way is this one coming true. You have a gorgeous mate and a beautiful daughter. You will be coming home to them. I promise you that. No brother of mine is going down that way."

Nico watched as Phoenix turned and walked back to the kitchen. Well shit, he hoped Phoenix had a good plan, because he hadn't come up with anything yet.

Once breakfast was done, Nico and Phoenix got ready to head back over to Angel's. Nico threw a packed bag on the bed and grabbed his bag filled with all of his other gear, adding it to the pile. "When will you be back?" Jenna asked, her eyes wet with unshed tears.

Sitting down on the bed, Nico pulled her between his legs. "It's going to be at least a couple of days. We found several facilities where the General is holding more women, including what looks like a main building that has a number of women in it. We are thinking that is where he breeds them, before shipping them out to the other places to be monitored by scientists. RARE is hitting the main facility; the council is handling all of the rest. We can't wait, Jenna. We have to hit hard and fast before he realizes we are on to him and he moves everyone."

A tear slipped free as she pulled him closer to her. "Be safe," she whispered. "Come home to me. Please come home to me, Nico."

Standing, Nico cupped her cheek and leaned forward to kiss her softly on the lips. "I will, mate. I will."

After one last kiss, he turned around and grabbed his bags, leaving the bedroom and heading to the door. He stopped when Lily came running after him, yelling for him. Nico dropped both bags and reached down, scooping her up and holding her close. "I love you, Daddy," she said, wrapping her arms around his neck. "Don't worry, I will take care of Mommy. And you will come home…but someone else won't."

Nico froze, "Who, Lily? Who won't come home?"

Lily just shook her head, whispering, "I don't know. It's too fuzzy."

Phoenix appeared behind Lily with both of his bags in one hand and Hunter by his side. Reaching down, he ruffled Hunter's hair. "We gotta go, cub." Hunter looked up at him, his eyes full of tears. "You will be fine, buddy. You stay here with Jenna until I get back."

"You will come back, too, Phoenix," Lily told him. "You think you won't, but you will."

Nico and Phoenix looked at each other. *Angel*, they both thought at the same time. Shit, they were going to have to watch her closely. There wasn't anything Angel wouldn't do for the people on her team. They were her family. Nico and Phoenix knew she could connect with them easily and they would not even know it had happened. She was that good. She probably already knew everything that they knew, and she wouldn't hesitate to put herself in Nico's place, allowing herself to be caught instead of him. But there was no way in hell they were leaving her behind.

They knew anyone on the team would have taken Nico's place if they could have, but Angel was the only one with the ability to connect to them without them knowing and pull out the exact information she needed. When Nico told everyone about his vision, he had neglected to tell them exactly where he was standing when he was shot and taken. But if Angel had wanted to know, she could have easily found out. She could be where she needed to be to take the shot for Nico. Because even though Nico knew where he was going to be at the time, he knew he could not avoid it. There was a reason he was in that spot, so when the time came, he would be there again. But he would not allow Angel to take his place. That was not going to happen.

33

The team was back in the basement conference room at Angel's house. They had been throwing around ideas for hours on how to infiltrate the large facility and free all of the women, and finally had it narrowed it down to one, along with a backup plan. The problem was, they had no idea how many guards they were up against. With the building having twenty-three women being held in it, they assumed the number of guards was at least half that. They needed the element of surprise on their side.

The facility they were infiltrating was in the Appalachian Mountains, on the Shenandoah Mountain in Virginia. They had decided to have pilots fly them in and drop them about ten miles out. They would have to beat feet all the way in, but they could do it. Phoenix was going to have to triple the amount of explosives he normally took on a mission if he was going to demolish the entire place, but he was looking forward to it. Women were meant to be cherished, not raped and forced to have babies. It made his blood boil to think about what they were going through.

RARE had every confidence that they could get in, get the women and get out, but the problem they were coming up against was how to get that many women to safety afterwards. They didn't know what kind of shape the women were in and could not expect them to run all of the way down the mountain. Which meant, they were either going to have to make the extraction point closer, or figure out something different.

Jaxson was the one that came up with the plan. Angel was the one that had to make the call to Chase. When Chase showed up at her home forty-five minutes later, she took him downstairs with the others. She explained everything that was going on, from the information they found on the computer at the place Flame and Janie were held, to the council having enforcers invading the smaller facilities and RARE taking on the biggest one. Then, Angel and her team laid out their plan for him and explained exactly what they needed him to do to help with the extraction. Chase sat there quietly for a few minutes taking it all in, and then just got up and walked out of the room.

Angel found him upstairs in the kitchen, hands clenched tightly into fists, a muscle ticking in his jaw as he stared at her when she walked in. He was obviously pissed off.

"Chase?" she inquired softly.

All of a sudden, he let out a roar and the kitchen table went flying across the room, hitting the wall and landing in pieces on the floor.

"I am not sitting down at the bottom of a fucking

mountain waiting for my mate while she is at the top of it fighting for her life and the lives of her team and twenty-three women. Not gonna fucking happen. Do you understand me, Mate?" he growled.

"Back off, Chase. I can't take you with me and you know it. RARE is going in and only RARE. I am not going to risk the lives of my team just because you have a problem with me doing my job. I have been doing it for years without you, and you are not going to go in and hold my fucking hand now. Do you understand me, Mate?" she growled right back. Chase's chest heaved as he glared at her, but there was no way Angel was backing down. "I need you as far up that mountain as you can get with those SUVs, Chase, not at the bottom of it. I can get the women to you, but I need you there waiting for me. I am asking you for your help. I am trusting you to do this for me."

Chase swallowed hard as he watched her. Then, he grabbed her and yanked her to him, covering her mouth with his. Threading his fingers through her hair, he ground his mouth against hers, and she moaned as he tangled his tongue with hers. Just as quickly, he pulled back breathing heavily. "When do you need me there?"

"I have to talk to the council enforcers to see when they will be ready to go. For this to work, we all need to strike at the same time. I will call you." Angel pulled him back down for one more quick kiss, before pulling away and heading back downstairs.

"Angel," Chase called out. She stopped and glanced back up at him. "Stay safe," he ordered.

Angel nodded, sending him a jaunty wave, before

turning around and heading the rest of the way down the stairs.

"He's in," she told her team when she entered the room where they were waiting patiently. "Nico, get on the phone with the council enforcers and get them here to go over the final plans. We need to be in position tomorrow night."

34

By the time Storm and Ryker arrived, RARE had their final plan fine-tuned and ready to go. Once they knew what the council had planned on their end, Nico would contact the pilot to set up the drop point and time, and Angel would contact Chase about the extraction point.

As the council enforcers took their seats, the team filled in the rest of the chairs. "What do you have for us?" Angel asked them.

"We had to enlist the help of shifters in territories close to the facilities," Storm told them. "Sixteen places is a lot to hit all at once. It would spread our enforcers too thin. We need some to stay behind to protect the council."

"That's understandable," Angel said. "When is everyone set to go in?"

"Tomorrow morning, 6 a.m."

"We do not go in during the day," Angel said, shaking her head. "We always hit at night. You know this."

"I know," Storm replied, "but we didn't have a choice

this time. The council wants the women out now. They refuse to wait."

"We asked the council for help this time, not the other way around. They don't tell us what to do. We go in at night. It is too dangerous to go in during the day. Do they want to lose shifters?" Angel was pissed. Who the hell did they think they were taking over? Oh yeah, the fucking council. They didn't have to answer to anyone.

"I'm sorry, Angel," Storm said. "It's all set up for tomorrow morning at 6 o'clock. I work for the council. To me, what they say goes."

"Get out," Angel growled at them. "We will hold a vote without either of you in the room. I will send one of the team members up to tell you our decision. Wait on the front porch." That was her way of letting them know that they were not a part of her team. They worked for the council. They were loyal to the council. Her team was loyal to her. But unlike the council, Angel would not make this kind of decision on her own. All of the team would have a choice.

Storm apologized again, and then she and Ryker left the room and went upstairs. As soon as Angel knew they were out of the basement, she got up and shut the door, locking them all in the soundproof room. "Talk to me."

"Doesn't look like we have a fucking choice," Phoenix ground out. "I prefer to hit the facility at night, but if we don't go in with the rest of them, it gives General Dick-head a chance to move the women."

"He's right," Rikki said, sighing in frustration. "As much as I hate it, I say we get dropped in at midnight. That will give us time to get up the mountain and scope everything out. Trace and I can pick our trees to camp out in, and get up in them so we will be camouflaged while it's still dark."

Nico nodded. "I agree with them. We have to do this. We don't have a choice. We need to get those women out of there."

"I'm in," Jaxson said. "It doesn't matter if we like it, those women don't deserve what's happening to them. They need us."

Trace nodded his agreement. "Let's do this."

Angel took a deep breath. Against her better judgment, she agreed with her team. "Phoenix, go tell them we will be ready to go in at 6 a.m. Nico, call and set it up with the pilots. I will get ahold of Chase. He is going to have to fly in and rent vehicles now. There is no way they will get there in time otherwise. Jaxson, set him up with SUVs and have them waiting for him to pick up when he gets there."

As Phoenix pulled the door open, he said, "I've got a bad feeling about this, boss."

"Yeah," Angel said, a feeling of trepidation running down her spine. "Me, too." Grabbing her cell phone, she made the call to Chase.

Worry filling him, Phoenix headed up the stairs and out onto the front porch to talk to the enforcers. What he found was Storm. She turned to face him when he walked out. "We will be at the facility at 6 a.m.," he told her, and turned to leave, having nothing else to say.

"Wait."

Phoenix paused, turning back with his eyebrows raised. "Yeah?"

"Phoenix, please," she said.

"Just let it be," he told her. "It's done." As he moved away again, she reached out and grabbed his arm. Phoenix shrugged her off and turned back. "Look, Storm, it would never work. I want someone who is loyal to me. Not to my team, to me. Someone I can trust. You proved that someone isn't you."

"Dammit, Phoenix," she growled, "Angel asked a question and I answered it. Don't give up something we could have just because of that."

"Am I your mate?"

"What?" she asked in surprise.

"Am. I. Your. Mate?" Phoenix ground out.

"Well, no."

"Then once again, don't waste my time or yours. I refuse to settle for anything less than the woman I plan on spending the rest of my life with. I'm tired of the endless fucking with no emotions. I want something real, and I will remain faithful to that woman now, even though I haven't found her yet. You're a shifter, Storm. Why would you even think of settling for less than your intended mate?"

Storm turned around and walked to the door. Looking back at him, she said, "I have waited for my mate for over one hundred years, Phoenix. I would have liked you to be that mate, but you aren't. It gets lonely waiting."

As the door closed behind her, Phoenix took in a deep breath. Yeah, he had originally been attracted to Storm, but he had known she was not for him. Not long term, and long term was all he wanted now. He wasn't wasting his time on anything less than the real deal.

35

The team spent the rest of the time cleaning their weapons and getting ready for the rescue mission. Nico debated on saying something to Angel about what he suspected she might be planning, but decided to wait. He could be wrong, and if he was, he didn't want to raise her suspicions. Phoenix agreed with him.

Phoenix was back in the armory that Angel had in the corner of her basement loading up on all of the explosives he needed. It was going to take three bags this time instead of the normal one, but that was fine. Nico had agreed to carry one of them until they got to the building and Phoenix took off on his own to set up. He was going to put them all in place under the cover of the night. No way in hell was he waiting until dawn and risk being seen.

Trace was cleaning his sniper rifle and Rikki had gone out back to sight hers in. There was a reason she never missed her mark. Her rifle was her baby, and it was always cleaned and sighted in. Always.

Jaxson sat in front of his computer. His weapons were

ready to go and he was in the process of getting the vehicles ready for Chase and his enforcers to grab as soon as they got off their plane.

Once everything was packed and ready to go, they geared up and headed out to the airport. On the plane, they went over everything twice. They were in the zone and ready to rock and roll. The team bailed out of the plane over the Shenandoah Mountains and landed near the ten-mile mark they had set. Then, they all took off under the cover of the dark at a fast clip up the mountain toward the building where the women were being kept.

When they were a couple of miles out, they slowed down and moved in silently. It was very important that they did not attract any unwanted attention this early in the mission.

When they were close to a mile from the facility, Nico shouted telepathically, *Find cover now! Chopper coming in fast and low!* Quickly, they all slipped into the shadows under bushes and behind trees. Soon, they heard the helicopter, and then it was flying over them and landing on a ridge near the building. As they watched, the General himself exited the chopper and climbed down the steep ridge moving toward the building.

Let me take him out now, Rikki demanded raising her rifle, but he was already inside before she could get a bead on him. *Dammit!*

Proceed with the plan, Angel ordered. *Do not deviate from the plan. I mean it. Now, fan out, but be very careful. Phoenix, get your toys set quickly. Everyone else, surround the building. I want eyes on that place now. Trace and Rikki, find your homes and stay there.*

Phoenix grabbed his third bag from Nico and moved

silently closer to the building, watching carefully for trip wires, motion lights, and guards. He was going to get all of his toys hidden around the outside of the building, and once all of the women were out, he was going to light this place up like the Fourth of July.

Trace and Rikki quickly found their spots. Trace went around to the other side of the facility where the back entrance was, and Rikki found the perfect perch in a tree near the ridge where the helicopter was sitting up above the building. She was going to pick the bastards off one-by-one when they ran for the helicopter.

Angel moved to the back of the building, going in a different direction than Trace had. Nico was going to scan the south side of the building while Jaxson checked out the north side. RARE wanted all of their bases covered, and to do that, they needed to know where every door and window was in the place. They were also hoping to find out where the guards were posted on the outside of the building and what their routines were. That way they could easily take them out before moving into the building later.

Two guards at the back door, Trace said. *No windows back here. Guards are smoking and jacking around.*

One guard over here on this side, Nico told them. *Walking the perimeter back and forth. Five windows. Three on the first floor, all with bars. Two on the second without. Nobody in them.*

One guard on this side, too, Jaxson said. *Same routine. Two windows on the first floor, two on the second. Bars on all of the first-floor ones, not the second. Have to be a spider monkey to get up the wall. Good thing Phoenix isn't the only one with toys.* He paused for a second, and then continued, *I see move-ment in both windows on the second floor.*

Movement up front, Rikki let them know. *Two more guards coming back out. Two windows on the bottom floor here with bars, two on the top without. Left window has one woman. Right window looks like some sort of lab.*

Okay, spider monkey, get up on the roof and tell me what you see, Angel said. Jaxson slipped his special gloves on, along with the special covers that went over his shoes. When the guard turned around and was headed away from him, Jaxson sprinted across to the building and was halfway up it within seconds. He stopped and glanced down at the guard, but the dumbass was oblivious to what was happening just above him. Jaxson quickly moved the rest of the way up the wall and peered over the edge, before pulling himself over and onto the roof.

He dropped low and swiftly ran around the flat rooftop, checking it out. *All clear, boss. It's a flat top. Open. No guards up here. I don't see any cameras anywhere, either. I need to get in that building. I want what's on his computers.*

Can you get in from up there? Angel asked.

Yeah, there's a door. I'm going to sneak in and see what I can find. Jaxson stripped off his gloves and feet covers, stored them back in his pack, and moved toward the door. Cautiously, he opened it and silently moved down the flight of stairs to the second floor. There was a small window in the door, and he peered through it carefully. When he didn't see any movement, he slowly inched the door open. As he did, a woman in a white lab coat walking down the hall glanced up and saw him. Her eyes widened, and she shook her head once. Jaxson quickly shut the door and watched as she walked past it, followed by a guard with a gun. He watched as the woman opened a door and the guard shoved her hard. She fell onto the floor and the guy followed her into the room, unbuckling his belt. No way was Jaxson staying put when a woman was about to be raped. He didn't care who she was.

Got a problem boss. Just about got made. A scientist saved my ass, but she's about to get hers taken by a guard. He has her cornered in a room. I'm taking him out.

You need back up? I can be in there in five.

Jaxson moved silently into the corridor. *She doesn't have five, Angel. I'm going in now.* He drew out his Glock and slowly pushed open the door that the woman had gone through. She was on the floor with the guard on top of her. He had shoved her skirt up and was pulling his pants down. She was struggling to get free when she saw Jaxson, but instead of giving his presence away, she made sure the guard's attention was on her by reaching up and raking her nails across his face. "You fucking bitch," he roared, wrapping his hands around her neck and squeezing tightly.

Jaxson quickly moved up behind him and snapped his neck. As he pulled the guard off of her, the woman gasped for breath clawing at her throat. "Calm down," he said softly. "It's going to be okay, calm down and breathe."

Pulling deep breaths of air into her lungs, she started coughing. Her eyes filled with tears as she watched him. "Who are you?" she croaked, as she struggled to sit up.

"Someone who is getting you out of here," Jaxson responded, placing an arm around her shoulders to help her.

Glancing around while he waited for her to catch her breath, Jaxson realized he was in a lab. Just where he needed to be. Standing, he grabbed the guard by his ankles and started dragging him toward a desk.

"Wait," the woman said, rising to her feet and crossing the room. "Put him in here." She opened a closet door and held it for him, shutting it once he had dumped the guard in.

"What's your name?" Jaxson asked her.

"Becca," she rasped, her hand going to her throat again. "My name is Becca. Look, if you are here to help, we need to get the women out of here. We have to hurry."

"How many women are here?" Jaxson asked her.

"There were over twenty, but he's been moving them. Something happened and he's relocating everyone," she whispered hoarsely. "Now there are only nine left."

"Why are you still here?" Jaxson wanted to know.

"Because they haven't taken the time to kill me yet," she responded bitterly.

"Kill you?"

"When you refuse to do things they tell you to, or you try to protect the women, they kill you," she said, running a shaking hand through her long, dark hair. "The General is here to make sure the rest of the women are ready for transfer. There's a young girl here. She's barely seventeen. I locked her in her room tonight and refused to let any of the men near her. Then, the General showed up. He told me that if I wouldn't unlock her door, that I could take her place. I told him I had to come to the lab to get the keycard."

Jaxson nodded. "Do you have it? We will need it to get her out soon."

Becca nodded, tears slipping down her cheeks. "You really are going to get them out of here? Thank God."

Seems the General knows something is up. The lady says there are only nine women left. He is here to make sure they are ready to be transferred to a new location, Jaxson told the team.

Can you do what you need to do quickly so we can move in, Jax? Angel asked.

Glancing around the room Jaxson found two computers. *Yeah, I will get it done. Give me ten minutes.*

"I need to get all of the information off of the computers quickly," he told Becca, removing two USB flash drives from his pocket. He hesitated briefly when she held her hand out for one, and then handed one of them to her. Jaxson downloaded everything from one of the computers, as she did from the other. He was trusting one of the scientists in this whole fucked up operation, but she had proven herself so far, and he was not leaving her here.

"I'm done," she told him a few minutes later handing it back to him.

"Let's get out of here," he said, as he finished up on his end.

I'm done. We are going to collect the women on this floor and head down. Get ready. Quietly, they moved out of the lab and down the hall. Jaxson stopped at the first door and went to open it. Becca grabbed his arm, shaking her head. Moving around him, she glanced up and down the hall. Then she reached over and knocked twice, waited, and knocked once more. Using a key card, she opened the door. A woman slipped quickly out, following them as Jaxson and Becca moved down the hall. They stopped at six more doors doing the same thing. When they headed over to the door leading downstairs, Jaxson grabbed Becca and whispered, "You said nine women. Where are the other two?"

"First floor. There are two more guards, plus the General and his personal guard. The young girl is locked in one room and Serenity is in another. One of them got to Serenity and gave her something after she attacked him. I couldn't get to her in time. She's so full of drugs I don't think she is even lucid at this point."

"Give me the keycards to their rooms. I want you to take the rest of the women out the back door. Wait until I tell you to, then slip out. My team will be there, and they will keep you safe," Jaxson told her.

"But, what about you?"

He gave her a cocky grin. "I will catch up with you. You won't even know I'm gone."

She watched him in concern, but then seemed to realize that the women needed her more, and she finally nodded in agreement. They moved silently down the stairs to the first floor. Jaxson glanced quickly through the little window on the door. It was clear. "The rooms are toward the front," Becca whispered. "They will all be up there. One of the guards, the blond one, is telepathic. The other is a precog, but it is very random. Be careful of the telepathic one. He can warn the guards outside." Jaxson put his hand on Becca's shoulder to let her know he had heard.

I'm sending them your way, Trace. There are eight of them, including Becca, the scientist. There are two more in with the General still. One is a young girl, the other is someone named Serenity. She's heavily drugged and unable to move or defend herself. Phoenix, if you are done playing, I could use you in here.

You got it, he heard Phoenix respond. *I just unwrapped my last toy and am ready for the party.*

Hold off on that, boys, Rikki said. *Front door is opening. Shit, it's the General. He is carrying a woman. She's not moving. Such a tiny thing.*

Damn, that must be Serenity. He couldn't get into the other girl's room, Jaxson told them.

We can't wait any longer. Trace, take care of the guards in the back. Phoenix, get the women moving down the mountain to Chase. Rikki, take out anyone you can that is not a friendly, Angel ordered.

Done, Trace said.

"Go," Jaxson told the women. "Now!" Becca opened the back door, and they ran for the tree line. Jaxson waited until he saw Phoenix motioning for them to follow him, then he turned and ran to the front of the building that was now empty, except for the young girl pounding on the door of the room she was locked in. Running over, he unlocked it with the keycard and pulled her behind him toward the back door. Trace was waiting for them, and Jaxson pushed the girl to him.

Nico pulled the trigger of his Glock, hitting the guard on his side of the building, while Angel took out hers. Glancing around, Angel scanned the area, a bad feeling seeping into her bones. *Something is wrong. This is too easy.*

Suddenly, there was a loud shout, and an army of men came at them from the trees. Holy shit, there were so many of them. Rikki lay across the branch in her tree, one eye closed as she tracked bastards through the scope on her rifle, picking them off as quickly as she could. Phoenix came back around the front of the building shooting left and right, while Jaxson helped Trace defend the women in the back. Angel's throwing stars were hitting their targets as quickly as she could let them go.

When she ran out, she pulled out her gun and started shooting.

The General scrambled up the hill to the helicopter, Serenity in his arms. He had almost made it. Rikki tried to take the shot, but it wasn't there. Nico ran up the ridge, trying to catch the General and get to the woman. Rikki took two more shots before dropping her gun.

It was just like in Nico's vision. He was almost to the top of that fucking ridge. He was trying to get to the General who was carrying a very small woman. The General reached the helicopter, turning just as Nico scrambled over the top. The woman in his arms was blocking any shots to him.

Phoenix fought to get to Nico. The bastards were not taking his brother. He had Jenna and Lily waiting at home for him. Phoenix could not let it happen. But no matter how hard he fought to get through the army of men and get up the steep incline to Nico, he knew there was no way he would get there in time. It was all just how Nico had described it. Utter chaos. "No!" Phoenix screamed as he clawed his way up the hill. "Nico, run!"

Phoenix watched as a guard rushed at Nico, and Nico's blade sliced through the other guy's neck. He fell to the ground, leaving Nico standing wide open on the edge of the incline. Suddenly, Nico was falling down the incline toward Phoenix as he was shoved roughly from behind. Phoenix watched in horror when the bullet meant for Nico slammed into Rikki. What the fuck was she doing there? She was supposed to be up in a tree picking off the General's army.

Bright red blood spread across her chest and her pain-filled gaze met his. *Neither of you are expendable, my brother,* she whispered into his mind. *Love you both so much.* Then she was gone, the link severed as she fell to the ground.

Two men grabbed her roughly, picking her up and running swiftly to the helicopter with her, and throwing her inside. Just like that, the fighting stopped. As soon as the helicopter was safely gone, most of the General's men retreated. RARE quickly picked off the ones that were left, but they were all running on auto pilot now. Rikki was gone. Their little sister, the youngest of the group, had just sacrificed herself for the two brothers she loved more than anything in the world, and now she was gone.

36

"Let's go," Angel growled, her gaze raking over the dead bodies of the General's men around her. "We need to get to the extraction point." They took off down the mountain as fast as the women could move, and when they were far enough away she ordered, "Blow the fucker, Phoenix." Phoenix detonated the explosives and the building blew sky high.

It took them almost two hours to get to where Chase and his enforcers were waiting for them. Once there, they piled into the SUVs and headed toward home. Chase had asked where Rikki was, but Angel just clenched her jaw and shook her head, her blue eyes shining brightly with suppressed tears.

Nico still could not believe what had happened. Rikki had given her life for him. No, he would not believe she was dead. She was not dead, and they were going to find her. They were going to tear apart every fucking place associated with the General until they found her.

Pain filled his heart as he thought about the woman he

thought of as a little sister. Before Rikki joined RARE, she had no family. She was another foster kid that had slipped through the cracks, just like Phoenix. She hadn't told any of the team her whole story, just that she didn't have anyone and had ran away from her last foster family at the age of fifteen. She'd been on her own since then. Angel had done a thorough background check on her, just as she had on all of them, and Nico knew that she knew everything there was to know about Rikki, otherwise she wouldn't have hired her. But no one else knew the details of Rikki's life before RARE, and Angel respected her privacy.

Phoenix and Nico adopted Rikki right away. She had been a tough little thing with a chip on her shoulder. She was still tough, but she had attached herself to Phoenix and Nico and was learning to chill out more, even acquiring a sense of humor. She was the little sister they never had. The team was her family. Rikki had finally found a place she belonged, and she had finally found out what it was like to love and be loved. Before them, she hadn't really known what love was, but she loved her family more than life itself. And she loved Phoenix and Nico more than anyone, because they had taken the first steps in accepting her. They were there for her when fighting her personal demons had become too much, and she just needed someone to be there. She had spent many nights at their place, crashed out on their couch because she didn't want to be alone. She loved her family, but she lived for Phoenix and Nico.

Nico looked over at Phoenix where he sat with his elbows on his knees, his head in his hands. "We're gonna get her back, Phoenix," he growled. "We are going to bring her home."

Phoenix raised his head, and Nico saw the raw pain in his gaze. "She knew the plan, man. She knew I was going to take that bullet for you and get them to take me instead. How the fuck did she know?"

Looking back at them, Angel whispered, "The trash."

"What?" Nico asked, his eyes narrowing on her.

"The trash. After our meeting, she took the fucking trash out. I thought she was putting it in the dumpster. She had to have taken it home and found something that showed her what you saw and what you planned. Why didn't I catch that? Why the hell didn't I catch that?" she cried. Chase reached over and placed a hand on hers. He didn't know exactly what had happened, but he was slowly piecing it all together.

Fuck, Nico needed Jenna now. He needed his mate. He needed to hold her, and to let her shoulder some of this burden with him. To help take the pain away, just for a little bit. Then he was going hunting. They were all going hunting, and they would not stop until Rikki was back home where she belonged.

37

I t took them a full day to get home, even driving straight through, but there were too many of them to fly. When they pulled into the compound, Nico barely waited for the SUV to come to a stop, before he jumped out to head for home and Jenna.

"Nico, Phoenix," he heard Angel call. Nico paused, glancing back at her. "My house tomorrow. Be there as early as you can."

"Wait," a woman called out as she exited one of the vehicles. "You're Phoenix?"

Phoenix turned toward her, an eyebrow raised. "I am. Why?"

"Oh, God," another woman cried out, taking a step toward him. "I told her he was coming. I told Serenity he was coming for her."

"Serenity?" Phoenix asked, frowning in confusion.

"Serenity," the woman said. "Your mate." Phoenix stared at her blankly, wondering what the hell she was talking about.

"All of the women were being held upstairs, except Serenity and the young girl. They were downstairs," Becca said quietly. "I had locked the girl into a room so the guards couldn't get to her. One of the guards was pissed because he had tried to force himself on Serenity, but she had just found out about you from Ashley the night before. Ashley told her that her mate, Phoenix, was coming for her. That everyone was going to be rescued soon. Serenity told the guard there was no way he was touching her because she was not going to have her mate smell his filth on her. She sliced his chest open with her claws. He beat her and then drugged her and shoved her in one of the rooms downstairs."

Phoenix just stood there staring at the women. He had a mate? God, he wanted a mate. He remembered the tiny woman with long dark hair and delicate features that the General had held in his arms on his way to the chopper. It had to have been Serenity. She had been drugged and at that point he wasn't sure she had even known what was going on around her. He had just gotten a quick glimpse of her because he had been so focused on getting to Nico. Damn, if only he had known. He would have done what? He couldn't get to Nico. He would not have been able to get to Serenity either. But it didn't matter. She was his, and he had let the General take her.

"My mate?" he growled. "You have got to be fucking kidding me! I lost my little sister AND my mate?"

Phoenix swung around and slammed his fist into the car window next to him, shattering it. As he pulled his bloody hand back, he looked over at the women, and cursing darkly again, he walked over and got into one of the SUVs. He had to get out of there. Had to be alone. His mate. His beautiful little mate. So tiny. She had been waiting for him to come rescue her. He had lost Serenity and Rikki. That sick prick had them both. Phoenix had failed them. He tore out of the compound, blood pouring from the gashes in his hand. All he could think about was his mate and his sister.

They were all going to die. Every last bastard that worked for the General had just signed their own death warrant, and he was the mother fucking Grim Reaper.

Nico watched Phoenix leave, knowing he had to let him go this time. How much more could the guy take? It was all so jacked up. "Go be with your mate and child," Angel told him softly. "He has to work this one out on his own. Be there early tomorrow."

Nico nodded, and with one more glance at the fleeing vehicle, he turned around and ran home. Jenna was there when he opened the door and he yanked her into his arms, burying his face in her neck. He was shaking, and he couldn't stop. She leaned back and looked up at him, questions in her eyes.

"It was Rikki," they heard a tear-filled voice say. They both turned to where Lily stood in the kitchen doorway. "I didn't know, Daddy. I'm sorry, I didn't know." She ran to him, her breath catching as she sobbed, and Nico scooped her up, holding her close. Her abilities were supposed to be a gift to her, not a burden. He didn't want her to feel like this.

He gently stroked her hair and whispered, "Yes, Princess, it was Rikki, but we are going to get her back."

Lily leaned back and looked at him. "And the pretty white wolf. You have to get her back, too."

She had to be talking about Serenity. As Jenna watched

in confusion, he said, "We will definitely be bringing Serenity home, too, Princess."

"No, not Serenity, Daddy. The other wolf. She's scared and wants her mommy. She needs to come home with Rikki." Now Nico was confused, too, but he promised Lily he would do what he could for all of them.

Nico spent the rest of the evening with his family. After they put Lily to bed, he and Jenna sat out back on the porch swing. He held her close, as he pushed the swing and told her about the mission. And then he told her about Rikki. About how much she had changed and opened up since she had first come to work for RARE. About how she used to always come over and hang out at Nico and Phoenix's and was the pesky little sister they'd never had. About what she had done for him so that he could come home to his family. And about how much he loved her, and was scared to death that she was not going to come home to them at all.

He also told her about Serenity and how it had to be tearing Phoenix apart that he had not been able to save Rikki, or his mate. A mate he hadn't even known he had.

Through it all, Jenna held onto him and just let him talk. Afterwards, they went inside and climbed into bed. Nico held Jenna, thanking God that she and Lily were home safe. He loved them both so much, and would do anything to keep them from the General.

The next morning, Nico got up while Jenna was still sleeping. He silently dressed and then leaned over to give her a quick kiss. Without opening her eyes, she whispered, "You bring them home, Nico. You find them and bring them home."

Nico nodded and gave her a hug, then went into Lily's

room and gave her a kiss and hug, also. "Rikki's hurting, Daddy, but Serenity is going to help her. She has a secret. And she's still waiting for Phoenix." Lily yawned and turned over, snuggling back into her covers to fall back to sleep.

Serenity had a secret? Nico headed out to ask Chase for a vehicle, but stopped when he saw Phoenix sitting in one in front of the house. Glad he was there, Nico went over and got in the SUV. Phoenix glanced at him, then turned the vehicle around and headed to Angel's. "Lily says Rikki's going to be okay. That Serenity has some sort of secret and is going to help Rikki." Nico said softly. "She also says Serenity is still waiting for you, Phoenix."

One lone tear fell down Phoenix's face. "Let's hope she doesn't have to wait too long," he rasped.

Pain. There was so much pain. She was on fire. The bullet had hit her closer to the shoulder than the chest, but it still hurt like a bitch. Rikki squeezed her eyes shut, breathing hard. She tried to shut out the pain, but it was just too much. When she felt a small hand reach over and touch hers, Rikki tried to jerk her hand away, but she couldn't move.

"It's okay. Let me help you," a voice whispered.

"Who…who are you?" Rikki gasped, as the hand moved from her hand up toward her shoulder.

"Shhhh," the voice whispered.

Rikki moaned when she felt white hot pain slam through her shoulder. It was utter agony. What in the hell was the woman doing to her? "That fucking hurts," she snarled.

"Not much longer," the voice huffed out. Suddenly, the pain started to recede, and then the hand fell away from her shoulder. The pain was not entirely gone, but it was more of a dull throb now.

"What did you do? Who are you?" she asked, slowly opening her eyes and looking around. She was in a dimly lit room, lying on a cot that was low to the floor. Close to her, she saw a woman sitting back against the wall, her long dark hair covering her face as she panted heavily.

The woman raised her head and gazed at her, her face pure white. Before she could respond, she fell over onto the floor and was out cold.

A door opened, and the General himself walked in. "Keeping secrets from me, Serenity?" he laughed cruelly. "We will see about that."

Make sure and visit my website for information on all of my books, and to sign up for my Newsletter where you will receive all of the latest information on new releases, sales, and more!

Website: **http://www.dawnsullivanauthor.com/**

I would love to have you join my reader's group, Author Dawn Sullivan's RARE Rebels, so that we can hang out and chat, and where you will also get sneak peeks of cover reveals, read excerpts before anyone else, and more!

https://www.facebook.com/groups/AuthorDawnSullivan sRebelReaders/

Dawn Sullivan

ABOUT THE AUTHOR

Dawn Sullivan has a wonderful, supportive husband, and three beautiful children. She enjoys spending time with them, which normally involves some baseball, shooting hoops, taking walks, watching movies, and reading.

Her passion for reading began at a very young age and only grew over time. Whether she was bringing home a book from the library, or sneaking one of her mother's romance novels to read by the light in the hallway when she was supposed to be sleeping, Dawn always had a book. She reads several different genres and subgenres, but Paranormal Romance and Romantic Suspense are her favorites.

Dawn has always made up stories of her own, and finally decided to start sharing them with others. She hopes everyone enjoys reading them as much as she enjoys writing them.

f facebook.com/dawnsullivanauthor

🐦 twitter.com/dawn_author

📷 instagram.com/dawn_sullivan_author

OTHER BOOKS BY DAWN SULLIVAN

RARE Series

Book 1 Nico's Heart

Book 2 Phoenix's Fate

Book 3 Trace's Temptation

Book 4 Saving Storm

Book 5 Angel's Destiny

White River Wolves Series

Book 1 Josie's Miracle

Book 2 Slade's Desire

Book 3 Janie's Salvation

Serenity Springs Series

Book 1 Tempting His Heart

Book 2 Healing Her Spirit

Book 3 Saving His Soul

Book 4 A Caldwell Wedding

Chosen By Destiny

Book 1 Blayke

Made in the USA
Coppell, TX
05 July 2024

34300698R00105